A Portal in Time
at the Chollar Mine

BRENDA K. FINDLEY, Ed.D.

With CARTER C. CHASSON

Thank you for visiting the Chollar mine
your tour guide Bill (Johnson) Findley

TABLE OF CONTENTS

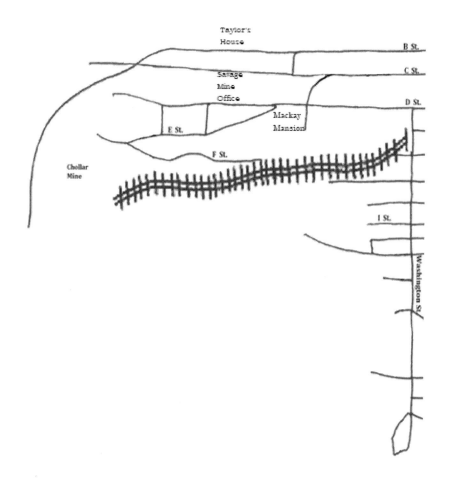

Taylor's
House

B St.

C St.

Savage
Mine
Office

D St.

E St.

Mackay
Mansion

F St.

Chollar
Mine

I St.

Washington St.

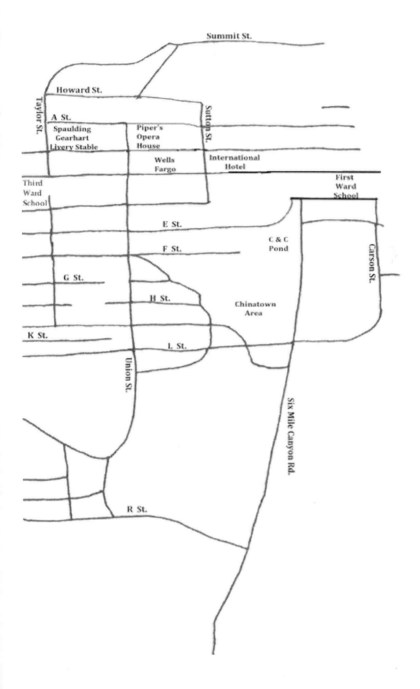

Summit St.

Howard St.

Taylor St.

A St.

Spaulding
Gearhart
Livery Stable

Piper's
Opera
House

Sutton St.

Wells
Fargo

International
Hotel

Third
Ward
School

First
Ward
School

E St.

C & C
Pond

F St.

Carson St.

G St.

H St.

Chinatown
Area

K St.

L St.

Union St.

Six Mile Canyon Rd.

R St.

V

PROLOGUE

Bill Johnson stood at the furthest end of the cavern and flipped the light switch to the "off" position. Four hundred and fifty feet from the mine's entrance, there was no hint of light from the outside. The darkness was complete. In the black silence, the visitors stood perfectly still. Everyone was afraid of taking a step in the wrong direction. Except for Bill, most of them were holding their breath, without even realizing it.

Three or four seconds later (although it seemed much longer), Bill said, "This is what it was like when a gust of wind came through the mine and blew out the miners' candles."

Waiting in the dark, the visitors heard the rasping sound of a lighter. A flame sprang to life, and Bill touched it to the candle. The entire group collectively sighed with relief when they could see again.

"It's amazing, isn't it? How much light a single candle emits?" Bill asked.

The visitors nodded in agreement. They almost always did. Bill conducted several tours of the Chollar Mine every day, and he never tired of telling the story of mining in Virginia City, Nevada. He loved the history of the town and the people in it. When he talked of the bonanza days of the 1800s, it sounded like he had been there just the other day, working alongside the miners. His enthusiasm and his friendly nature made him a favorite with the mine's visitors.

At the end of each day, Bill was exhausted, but content. His wife, Becky, had passed away four years earlier, so he spent most evenings by himself, watching gold-mining reality shows on television while he ate microwavable frozen dinners. Sometimes, he headed over to one of the saloons and had a drink with a few friends. It was a steady sort of life, and Bill liked it that way. He did his laundry on Saturday mornings and went shopping for his groceries on Sunday. He wore the same battered hat every day because it was his favorite, and when it finally wore out, he planned to replace it with another one just like it. Bill's life was predictable and satisfying, and he hoped it would always stay this way.

Chapter 1

Virginia City

It was the first full day of their vacation, and it should have been perfect. The sun rose promptly at 4:45 that morning, and there wasn't a cloud in the sky. The Taylor family had flown into Reno the day before, and after spending the night in a motel, they were excited about celebrating the Fourth of July in Virginia City. The morning air was crisp, and the mountains were beautiful. There was no hint of trouble when they headed out to the big SUV they had rented at the airport the night before. It *should* have been a perfect day.

"I call dibs on the 'regular' back seat!" twelve-year-old Natalie called out to her brothers, Alexander and Benjamin. All three of the Taylor children had brown hair and blue eyes, but only Natalie's hair was curly. She shaved it close on both sides of her head, but always left the section in the middle long enough for a French braid. She loved to swim and claimed that her hair cut helped her swim even faster, but her mother, Mary, thought it was more likely her way of expressing herself.

"I call dibs, too!" shouted Natalie's older brother, Alex. Just one year older than Natalie, he was super-smart and took accelerated classes at school. He was also a decent soccer player.

Lately, he had been completely unpredictable. Some days he could be the best older brother in the world, but other days he seemed to enjoy tormenting his siblings. It looked like today was going to be a tormenting day, because he picked up Benjamin, their six-year-old brother, and deposited him at the back end of the car, away from the 'regular' back seat.

Frowning, Benjamin stuck out his lower lip. "That's not fair! Why do I always get the back-back seat? I want to sit in the regular back seat!"

Sighing, their mother said, "Ben, you can sit in the back-back seat on the way to Virginia City. Alex will sit in the back-back seat this evening when we come back."

"Hey! Why can't Natalie sit in the back-back seat this evening?" asked Alex.

"You will sit in the back-back seat, young man, because you just picked up your brother without his permission. You know the rules. Benjamin gets to be in charge of his own body. Now, everybody, get in the car. No more bickering. I'm ready to get this party started! Where's your father?"

Thomas Taylor, the children's father, was running late. He was never late for work, but vacations were a different story. Thomas Taylor did not believe in hurrying while he was on vacation.

"Thomas!" Mary called out to the open door of their motel room. "Come on! We're waiting!"

Alex and Natalie groaned when their father emerged from the room. Wearing a short-sleeve button-down shirt, a pair of plaid shorts, white athletic knee-high socks, and ratty old sneakers, he looked like the goofiest dad in the world. An empty canvas backpack sagged against his back.

"We'll have to act like we don't know him," Alex said.

Natalie and Benjamin both laughed, while their mother tried not to smile. "Maybe we can get something else to wear while we're in Virginia City. I've heard they have Old West clothes you can buy, or you can even rent them for the day."

"I want some cowboy clothes!" Benjamin exclaimed.

Joining in, Natalie said, "I'd like to get a hat. Can we get hats?"

When he finally arrived at the car, Thomas climbed into the front passenger seat. Pulling the door shut, he asked, "What's this? Do we need hats? Did we bring hats? Should I go back in and get hats?"

"No!" his entire family said, in unison. If Thomas went looking for hats, there was no telling how long it would take him to come back to the car.

"I think we can splurge today," Mary said. "We can get hats in Virginia City, and maybe a few other things, too."

Putting the car in gear, she pulled out of the motel parking lot. Everyone else turned on their electronic devices and focused on their screens. The Taylors' Nevada vacation had finally begun.

"The wheels on the bus go round and round," Mary sang, as they drove along the winding mountain road that led to Virginia City.

She was trying, unsuccessfully, to get her family to join in. Her husband was no help at all. He sat in the front seat, hunched over, completely focused on the map he had downloaded just before they left the motel.

"I'm thinking we should start at the north end of town and work our way south. Then we have lunch. After that, we go to the Chollar Mine for a tour, and then come back up through town, going north. What do you think?" he asked, looking up at Mary.

"Round and round, round and round," she sang, smiling at him.

"Do you think it's Ch-ollar Mine with a 'ch' sound, or K-ollar Mine, with a 'k' sound?" he asked.

Mary gave up on the bus, and its wheels. She stopped singing and said, "I think it's K-ollar, with a 'k' sound, and we can explore the town whichever way you'd like." Raising her voice enough to be heard in the back-back seat, she said, "It's a shame my children are such party poopers!"

There was no response, so Mary turned on the radio and settled in for the rest of the twenty-minute drive. Natalie watched the curves in the road get tighter and tighter as they climbed the mountain, and then suddenly she could see Virginia City laid out in front of them.

"Look!" she exclaimed. "There it is!"

The car rounded another curve, and the town disappeared from sight.

"Just keep watching. You'll see it in a second," she said.

A moment later, the town came back into view. "There! Isn't it pretty?"

"Wow!" exclaimed Alex. "That's pretty cool! You can see the whole town from here!"

Everyone watched as the town got closer, until finally, they arrived. Mary slowed the car and they all started looking for a parking spot.

"There's one!" Natalie said, pointing to an open spot in a small parking lot. "Right next to the fudge shop. That'll be easy to remember!"

"Looks good to me!" her mother said, as she maneuvered the car into the vacant parking spot. When she put the gearshift into 'Park' five seatbelts clicked open and everyone climbed out of the car, taking a moment to stretch. Benjamin was the last to emerge, and his eyes never left the video game he was playing. He bumped his head on his way out, but he barely noticed.

He did take notice, though, when his father said, "No, sir. We are not bringing electronics with us today. All electronics, including cell phones, are going to be locked up in the car. We are going to have real-life experiences today."

Benjamin's face fell, and all three of the children groaned

"Come on, now," their mother said, "your father and I are in complete agreement about this. All electronics are going to stay in the car while we're in Virginia City. You can play with them on the way back to the motel."

While Mary paid the parking lot fee, Thomas collected all the gaming devices, cell phones, and smartwatches, and locked them in the center console of the car.

"Safe and sound," he said, turning the key in the lock. "Now, let's go have some non-electronic fun!"

While Benjamin scuffed his shoes and pouted over the loss of his video game, Alex moved closer to his mother and whispered, "Can we stop at a clothing store first?"

Mary winked at him, and then casually asked the group, "How about if we start by looking at some hats?"

"A new hat would be nice," said Thomas.

"And I was thinking we could check out the selection of Old West clothes, and maybe get our picture taken at the Historic West Photo Shop," she continued, smiling at her husband as she slipped her arm through her his. "What do you think? Can I interest you in some Old West clothes, cowboy? Maybe a pair of boots? You would look so handsome."

"Only if I can get a hat, too," Thomas laughed, pulling her a little closer.

An hour later, he and the boys looked like ranch hands from the Old West, and all the Taylors had new hats. They strolled along the boardwalk, watching out for the places where the boards were slightly misaligned, and listening to the creaking sounds beneath their feet. There were people everywhere, but "old-time" manners seemed to prevail here. Everyone smiled and nodded to each other as they passed.

They saw several people who were wearing clothes that looked like they were from the Civil War era, and they watched them in fascination. The town felt like it had been partially frozen in time. The narrow doors that led to each store along the boardwalk, and the tall glass windows with store names etched in gold lettering, magnified the effect. They saw cowboys and soldiers, and women who were wearing dresses with beautiful hooped skirts.

Scattered among them were a few old miners with their pack mules, and an occasional lawman.

"Howdy, folks," said a man sporting a big gold star as he passed them on the boardwalk.

"Howdy!" responded Alex, grinning.

They continued their stroll down the boardwalk, stopping to look in the various stores along the way, until Mary exclaimed, "Oh my goodness! Look at the adorable dress in the window of that shop! It looks like it would fit you perfectly, Natalie!"

"Uh, Mom, I'm good with just the hat," Natalie said, grimacing.

"Oh, come on! Humor me. It would be fun if you were wearing Old West clothes, too, like your brothers. Let's at least go have a closer look at it."

"OK," Natalie said reluctantly, throwing desperate looks at her brothers. She mouthed the words "help me," but Alex was clutching his stomach while he silently laughed at her, and Benjamin was busy peering in the window of the shop next door.

"Come in and turn around for me," Mary called from inside the store, holding up the dress on its hanger. It had a cream-colored background with a pink rose floral pattern, and there was a white ruffle along the bottom edge. Moving slowly, Natalie complied.

"Won't the white ruffle at the bottom get dirty?" she asked, hopefully.

Her mother held the dress against her back. "Just as I thought! It's not so long that it will touch the ground, and it looks like it will fit you perfectly! Go to the dressing room and try it on."

Carrying the dress, Natalie walked slowly to the dressing room. She knew there was no hope of changing her mother's mind once she got that cheerful, excited look in her eyes. There was nothing to do but resign herself to the situation.

"You have to come out so I can see it!" her mother called, after Natalie had been in the dressing room for a few minutes.

"The neck is all scratchy," Natalie said, from behind the door.

"Well, come out here so I can see it. Maybe we can do something about the scratchiness."

Natalie exited the dressing room, wearing the dress and looking miserable.

"It's the price tag that's scratching your neck, Sweetie!" her mother said happily. "See? We'll take that off, and it'll be fine!" She turned to the sales clerk and said, "We'll take it—along with those two parasols over there. Can she wear the dress out of the store?"

"Sure thing!" the sales clerk replied. "Here's a bag so you can carry her other clothes."

"I knew it!" Natalie mumbled quietly, bracing for the inevitable comments from Alex and Benjamin.

"With the hat and a parasol!" her mother exclaimed as they exited the store. "Just look at you! Just look at all of you! We definitely need to get a picture made while we're here!"

"I think we need to make one more stop first," their father said, pushing the bag of Natalie's regular clothes into his backpack. "You need a dress, too. You're the only one who isn't dressed for the Old West."

"Yeah, Mom," Benjamin said. "You need a dress, too."

"Oh, well, I suppose you're right. Maybe we can find something that isn't too expensive."

"Now you're worried about that?" their father asked, as though he was surprised.

After pretending to glare at him for a second, Mary turned around and said, "I think we passed a shop just a little ways back…"

Like a line of geese, the Taylor family turned to follow her.

"You look bee-u-ti-ful in your new dress!" Alex called out from behind his sister.

"Bee-u-ti-ful!" Benjamin chimed in.

Natalie pretended she couldn't hear them.

"Bee-u-ti-ful!" Alex called out one more time.

"Knock it off!" ordered their father at the back of the line.

Natalie spun around, as though she was showing off her dress, and stuck her tongue out at her brothers.

10

"Here it is! Oomph!" Mary said, as Natalie bumped into her. "Natalie, will you please watch where you're going?"

"Sorry, Mom," Natalie said sheepishly, ignoring the giggling behind her.

Once they were inside the shop, Mary peered at the price tags on the dresses and then picked the least expensive one she could find.

"This will do nicely," she said, heading to the dressing room to try it on. When she stepped out, her husband whistled appreciatively.

"You look great in that dress!" he said. "Maybe you should wear Old West clothes every day."

"Oh, sure," she replied sarcastically. "I can picture it now. I'm wearing my hardhat and safety glasses on a construction site, explaining an architectural drawing while my long skirt is blowing in the wind. Or jogging! Imagine that! I don't know how women got anything done wearing clothes like this. But it is fun for today! Now let's go check out the rest of the town and get a picture taken!"

They spent the rest of the morning walking through town and stopping at various stores, getting admiring glances as they walked. When the town's whistle blew at noon, they stopped for lunch at a saloon. Inside, they shared a table with three men who were also dressed in the style of the Old West. The men explained they were members of a volunteer group of town historians who strolled the

11

boardwalk every day and spoke with people who were visiting, answering their questions and sharing the history of the town.

"That sounds like a fun job," Alex said.

"Yes, it is." one man replied. "We get to meet interesting people, and it's fun to step back in time, but we're all volunteers. This isn't a job that pays anything. We do it because we love the town, and we want to share its history with our visitors."

"We also love it when visitors like you join in the fun," said another man. "We hope you're having a good time!"

"Oh, we are," Thomas said, reaching for his wallet to pay the bill. "And now we're headed over to the Chollar Mine to get a tour."

"I'm sure you'll enjoy that," the third man said. "That's a good tour. Be sure you stop by one of the old-time photography shops, while you're here, and get a picture taken. They have some great background props, including authentic furniture and fixtures from the 1800s. The picture frame is nice, too. It'll be a great memento."

"It's on the agenda," Mary assured them. "Right after the mine tour."

When the Taylors were ready to leave, all three of the men scooted their chairs back and stood up. They waited politely while Natalie and her mother stepped away from the table.

"Thank you, gentlemen," Mary said. "We enjoyed your company very much!"

"Such nice manners," she said, as they walked towards the door. Looking back at Alex and Benjamin, she added, "I hope you boys were paying attention."

"Oh, great," Alex muttered to his little brother. "She'll be scheduling another 'Totally Perfect Manners' dinner for us pretty soon. Just what I was hoping for."

The Chollar Mine was several blocks away, and Benjamin talked the whole way.

"Those cowboy guys were really cool! And I like the horses, too. I never saw wild horses before. And the candy stores! Those were cool, too. And the popcorn store!"

Benjamin didn't seem to be waiting for anyone to answer him, so the family just listened to him talk as they made their way to the mine.

"I'm thirsty!" he said, finally taking a break from his non-stop chatter when they arrived at the gate to the Chollar Mine property.

"It's no wonder," his father said, "you've been talking for the last ten minutes straight! We'll get you some water soon."

As the family neared the entrance, a man with a big gray mustache greeted them. He was wearing a plaid shirt, worn-out jeans, and a weather-beaten leather cowboy hat.

"Howdy, folks! Welcome to the Chollar Mine! My name is Bill Johnson, and I am glad to see you. Beautiful day, isn't it?"

"Yes, it is," Thomas said as he extended his hand. "My name is Thomas Taylor, and this is my wife, Mary. Our children are Alex, Natalie, and Benjamin. Did you say Chollar Mine with a hard 'k' sound?"

Shaking hands with Thomas, Bill said, "It's nice to meet all of you, and yes, it's 'Chollar' with a hard 'k' sound."

"Got it," Thomas said. "Are we on time for the tour?"

"Yes, you are!" Bill answered. "You're actually a little early. We have time to do some gold panning before the tour starts, if you'd like."

"Please! Please! Please!" exclaimed Benjamin, jumping up and down.

"What do you say, Pop?" Bill asked. "We guarantee that every pan will have some gold in it, or you get another pan for free. I can't say how much until we pan it out, but you will definitely have gold that you can take with you when you're done."

Smiling, Thomas said, "Let's set up three pans so they all get to try it."

"Excellent!" Bill said. "There's nothing like the thrill of seeing that flash of gold in your pan. The trick is to swirl the water around fast enough to throw out the lightweight material, but leave the heavier stuff at the bottom. Gold will always be the heaviest thing in your pan, so as you're swirling the water around, your gold is sinking down to the bottom."

Bill handed Alex, Natalie, and Benjamin pans filled with dirt and water, and then took one for himself.

"Like this," he said, showing them how to move the pan in a circular motion, tilting it from side to side as the water swirled around.

"You make it look so easy," Alex said, wincing when the water slopped over the edge of his pan.

"No worries. You're doing just fine," Bill said, reaching over to help Alex with the tilt of his pan.

After a few minutes, all three of them were excited to see the 'color' they had caught in the crevices of their pans.

"Now we pick out the gold and put it in a vial, so you can take it home and show it to your friends. Congratulations! You did very well! You probably have enough gold here that you could pay for your lunch."

"That's so exciting!" Mary said. "Thank you!"

"It's my pleasure," Bill said. "I love everything about gold panning, and mining, and the history of this town. I'm glad to share it with you. Is everybody ready to start the tour now?"

Nodding, the boys put their vials of gold in their pockets. Natalie put her vial in her dad's backpack, since her dress didn't have any pockets. As they walked through the entrance to the mine, Bill stopped to point out the enormous timbers that supported the ceiling.

"You see those timbers? The first thing you need to know about those timbers is that some of them hang a little low. The second thing you need to know is that they are much harder than your head. You'll have to watch out, and hunch over a little in some places. Those timbers are part of a support system called square-set timbering, which is a basically a bunch of wooden cubes that make sure the ceiling and the sides of the mine don't cave in. An engineering genius named Philip Deidesheimer developed it. If it weren't for his invention, the mine might be unstable and the ceiling could collapse. He saved a lot of miner's lives, and he saved the mine owners a lot of money. Unfortunately, Philip was not a good businessman. It never occurred to him to apply for a patent, so even though his square-set timbering design was used in mines all over the world for the next sixty years, he never earned a single penny from it."

Taking a few steps further into the mine, Bill said, "Here's another interesting fact: did you know it used to be illegal to kill the rats that lived in the mines? Don't worry—there aren't any rats here today, but do you know why it was illegal to kill them back in the old mining days?"

All five of the Taylors shook their heads.

"It's because the rats were the early warning system for the miners. They would run out of the mine whenever they sensed danger, like the smell of smoke, or if an earthquake were about to hit. The miners relied on the rats to keep them safe, and to warn them when they needed to get out of the mine. Rats were the miners' best friends, back in the old days. Most miners even shared their lunch with them."

Seeing the expressions on their faces, Bill said, "I know! Right? But it was a smart thing to do."

"How often do you have earthquakes here?" Alex asked.

"We have minor earthquakes all the time in this part of the country. Usually we don't even notice them, but we do get a good-sized earthquake now and then," Bill said, as he walked a little further into the mine. "In fact, just last year, in May, there was a good one while I was in the mine."

"Wow!" Natalie exclaimed, "That must have been scary."

"It was definitely a memorable experience, but we had already closed for the day, so I was the only one here. And thanks to our friend Philip, there wasn't any damage to the mine."

A little further in, he pointed out some of the equipment displays, including a huge drill and a pump that kept water from accumulating in the shafts. As he called their attention to the streaks of silver still embedded in the walls of the mine, the ground beneath their feet seemed to shift a little. Everyone swayed and caught their balance, and then there was another shift, just a little bigger than the first one.

"You've got to be kidding," Bill said, standing with his legs far apart, waiting to see what would happen next. They all looked at each other, and for a few seconds, everything was perfectly still. Then, they heard a faint roaring sound in the distance that grew a louder with each passing second, as though it was closing in on them. Suddenly, a wall of noise hit them like a freight train, and the ground rippled beneath their feet.

"Run!" Bill shouted. "It's an earthquake! We need to get out of here as fast as we can. Head towards the entrance!"

Thomas, who had been the last in the line, turned, and was now leading the group. Natalie was right behind him. He reached back and grabbed her hand, pulling her with him. "Come on!" he shouted. "Everybody run!"

Dust started to fill the air. Dirt and small rocks fell from the ceiling above them, covering their shoulders and the tops of their heads. Natalie did her best to keep up with her father as he pulled her along, but the dust was choking her. She kept stumbling on the uneven surface of the mine floor, and she was afraid she would fall before they made it out. Her heart was pounding wildly in her chest, and she wanted to cry, but there was no time.

Alex was close behind his father and sister, but he had so much dirt in his eyes he could barely see them. He reached out to grab Natalie's hand, but couldn't quite reach her. Squinting, he did his best to follow her. He staggered as he ran, tripping several times over the ore cart rails.

At the back of the group, Bill scooped up Benjamin and carried him like a football under his arm. As he ran past Mary, he grabbed her hand and pulled her along with him. By the time they all reached the exit, dust had completely filled the mine and they were choking and coughing. Further back in the mine a few small rocks continued to hit the ground. They breathed in the fresh air and brushed the dirt out of their eyes—and then looked at their surroundings in amazement.

Everything outside the mine had completely changed. Nothing looked the same as it had just a few minutes ago. The roaring sound they had heard inside the mine was even louder now that they were outside. For several seconds they stood perfectly still, trying to make sense of what they were seeing.

Bill was the first to recover. "This isn't right. We need to go back!" he said.

"Go back where?" Thomas asked, in confusion. "Go back into the mine? Why would we do that? We just had an earthquake!"

Still holding Benjamin under his arm, Bill turned and took a couple of steps back towards the mine. He blinked and then set Benjamin down when he saw that a large ore cart filled with rocks had suddenly appeared on the rails, blocking their path. Stepping towards it, he tried to push it out of the way, but after just a few seconds, he knew he couldn't move it by himself. He turned to the Taylors, who were still stunned and following him in a daze.

"I'm going to need a hand with this, unless you want to see if we can squeeze around it."

Turning back to his task, he caught a flash of movement at the corner of his eye. He used his hand to shield his eyes from the sun, and he could just make out the shadowy shape of a man moving toward them. Everyone else turned to see what Bill was looking at. A moment later, the shadow man called out to them.

"What are you doing over there?"

Nobody said a word. They all stood there, wondering what had just happened to the universe.

"I dropped my pocket watch," Bill finally said. "We were trying to go back and get it."

"Your pocket watch?" the man asked, reaching up to adjust his hat. "That might be the dumbest lie I ever heard, so I'm going to ask you one more time. What are you doing here?"

"I was giving them a tour," Bill said, deciding to tell the man the truth.

"A tour?"

All of the Taylors nodded.

Stepping to one side of the tracks, the man said, "I'll give you ten seconds to get your tails out of here. If it takes you longer than ten seconds, I'll send for the sheriff and have you arrested for trespassing."

They all turned and hurried away from the mine, but Bill stopped to ask the man a question.

"Did you feel an earthquake?"

"Yes, I did," he answered, with a puzzled expression on his face. "It was a good one. Everyone in town felt it. They probably felt it in California, too. Haven't you ever been in an earthquake before?"

"Oh, yes," Bill answered, "but not very many like this one."

The man stared at Bill for a second, and then said, "Don't come back here without an invitation."

Chapter 2

What Day Is It?

Bill led the group away from the mine, stopping when they reached the street corner. They huddled together and stared at their surroundings. Teams of horses were pulling wagons up the hill, away from the mine, and an enormous chimney was belching black smoke into the sky. Down the hill, several more of the massive chimneys were also pouring out smoke.

"What's happening?" Natalie asked in a shaky voice. "I don't understand what's happening."

"We're trying to figure that out," her mother said. She wanted to reassure her daughter, but she was concentrating on her breathing, trying not to hyperventilate.

Alex whispered to himself, "Wake up! Wake up!" while his father simply stood there looking dazed.

Bill checked his watch and then looked carefully in every direction.

"Would you like to sit down?" Alex asked his mother. "You look a little wobbly."

"Maybe you could sit on one of those big rocks by the corner," said his father. Concern for his wife seemed to have snapped him out of his daze. "You do look a little pale."

Taking the suggestion, she moved closer to the rocks and sat down on one of them. She continued taking slow, deep breaths.

"If you think you might faint, you should put your head between your knees," Alex said authoritatively. He had recently completed most of the requirements for his Boy Scout First Aid Merit Badge. The only requirement left was "Demonstrate competency performing CPR." He had already made one attempt to pass the CPR test, but it didn't go very well. He was quite sure, though, about how to treat light-headedness.

His mother looked up at him with a little smile. "Thanks for the reminder, but I don't think I'm going to faint."

"How did they change everything so fast?" Benjamin asked.

"I don't know," his father replied. He continued to take in his surroundings. "It's almost like..." his voice trailed off.

Natalie raised her head, and they all watched as a wagon pulled by four horses went slowly up the hill in front of them. The horses strained against the heavy load of rocks and dirt in the bed of the wagon, and with every step they took, a new little puff of dust from the road joined the cloud around their hooves.

After the wagon passed, Alex asked, "Wasn't this road paved before we went into the mine?"

"I'm pretty sure it was," Natalie said, feeling disoriented and queasy.

"Do you think…," Alex said, faltering.

"I keep expecting to wake up," said his father.

"Me, too!" Alex said.

Bill cleared his throat. "I'm going to go up the hill and take a quick look around. Maybe I can find out what happened. If the rest of you want to stay here and wait for me, I'll be back in just a few minutes."

After everyone agreed they would wait while he checked things out, Bill turned and walked briskly up the hill. The Taylors watched him until he went around the corner and disappeared from sight.

Natalie and Alex looked at each other with similar expressions of disbelief on their faces. Neither one could make sense of what was happening.

Unconcerned by the situation, Benjamin watched a line of ants marching to and from their anthill. It seemed like such an ordinary thing that the rest of the family watched them for a while, too. Eventually, Alex looked away.

"Is anyone else hungry?" he asked.

"You're hungry?" his mother asked him. She was incredulous. "How can you be hungry?"

"Well, actually, I'm not sure," Alex said. "I might throw up, instead."

"I kind of feel the same way," Natalie said. "Maybe we have motion sickness from the earthquake."

Mary laughed, but then quickly shook her head, willing herself not to lose control.

Another few minutes passed, and nobody spoke. Benjamin eventually lost interest in the ants and started digging in the dirt with a stick. It seemed like they had been waiting a long time when Bill finally reappeared at the corner and made his way back to them.

"OK, folks," he said, as he rejoined the group, "I think I know what happened."

He held out a newspaper, and everyone crowded around to look at it. "I found this in a trashcan up on C Street."

"1869!" Alex exclaimed when he saw the date in the upper right-hand corner. "What the heck?!"

"Yeah," Bill said, "I had the same reaction. But, well… it might help you to know that something like this happened to me once before. Except that I was by myself that time, and it was a quick trip."

"Trip? Trip to where?" asked Natalie.

Bill pursed his lips for a moment and said, "I'm going to tell you exactly what happened, even though I know how it's going to sound. Please keep an open mind. This is the absolute truth, as best I know it."

He paused, and then said, "Do you remember I told you about the earthquake we had last May, while I was in the mine? What I didn't tell you is that I 'time-slipped' during that earthquake, and when I came out of the mine I was in the year 1868."

"You what?" Natalie asked.

"But you were at the mine this afternoon when we got there," Alex said, interrupting his sister. "How did you get back?"

"I got lucky, is what I did," Bill answered. "I didn't know what to do, so I hung around the mine, trying to figure something out. I figured out it was 1868 by listening to the miners talking to each other for a while. My watch had stopped, so I'm not sure exactly how long I was there, but I'm sure it was less than an hour." He held out his arm to show them the digital watch he was wearing. "See? It's stopped again. Just like last time."

He took the watch off and put it in his pocket. The Taylors watched his every move, waiting to hear what he would say next.

"The last time this happened, there was a strong aftershock earthquake about an hour later. I was still at the mine, so I ran back to the same place inside the mine, where the silver is showing through. When the earthquake stopped I went outside, and I was back in my own time–and my watch was working again. It was like time stood still until I came back. I couldn't figure out what had actually happened, and, to be honest, after a few days went by, I decided I must have dreamed the whole thing–until it happened again a few minutes ago."

Nobody said anything, so he continued, "I think there is some kind of wormhole in the Chollar Mine that lets us travel through the space-time continuum. We didn't move through space, because we're still in Virginia City, but it's pretty clear we've traveled through time. It's the Fourth of July here, too, but the year is 1869."

He let that sink in, and then said, "If I remember my history correctly, that means Ulysses S. Grant is the President of the United States, and the Civil War just ended three or four years ago."

He took a deep breath and slowly exhaled. There was a long silence while they all processed this information.

"So, you're saying that we just traveled through time, to 1869, through a wormhole?" Thomas asked.

"Yes. Exactly." Bill said, "I believe we traveled through the time portion of the space-time continuum. We didn't change locations, so it seems to me that we didn't travel through space. The wormhole we went through was probably more like a doorway than a hallway."

Natalie decided this would be a good time to sit down on one of the big rocks near her mother. She took off her hat and hiked up her skirt so she could put her head between her knees. Dirt from the brim of her hat slid off and landed at her feet. Seeing this, the rest of the family took a minute to brush off the dirt that was still on their hats and shoulders.

"OK," Thomas said, having taken time to think while he was brushing off his hat. "I understand what you're saying, even though I don't understand how it happened. But, if our time is on the other side of a wormhole doorway thingy, how do we go through it the other way, back to our own time?"

"I'm pretty sure we just step through the opening during an earthquake."

Mary spoke next, between measured breaths.

"So, there is a wormhole that starts at the Chollar mine, and ends up in a different time?"

"Right," Bill said. "That's what I think. Except I think the wormhole is usually closed off. I think earthquakes open it up. Like a hatch, or something."

"Like a portal," Alex said. He was still expecting to wake up, but he figured he could be helpful while he waited for that to happen.

"Yes! A portal," Bill replied. "On the other side of the portal is our time. On this side of the portal it's 1869."

Natalie lifted her head. "How are we supposed to get back to the right spot during the next earthquake? How are we supposed to know when the next earthquake is going to hit? And how are we going to get back into the mine?"

"I don't know how we're going to get back into the mine. We certainly can't do that right now. Even if there's a strong aftershock in the next few minutes, we can't get past the guard. The last time this happened, it was just me. I was just one guy who looked like a miner. This time, with an entire family, there's no way we could sneak in. And even if we could, how would we get past the ore cart that's blocking the entrance? I think we're probably stuck here until December 26th—which is the next earthquake I know about."

Everyone looked at him even more intently.

"How do you know there's going to be an earthquake on December 26th?" Thomas asked.

"I did some research on Virginia City earthquakes after what happened last May," Bill explained. "I remember the date because it was the day after Christmas. December 26th, 1869, at six o'clock in the evening."

"OK," Mary said, "it's good that you know that, but if we have to wait until December 26th, that's almost six months away! How are we supposed to survive until then? Not to mention the problem about how we're going to get inside the mine when December 26th finally gets here."

"Also not mentioning the problem about how we'll all be missing in our own time," Thomas said. "If we have to wait six months before we can go back, everyone will think we're dead!"

Bill took his hat off and ran his hand over his head. "I don't think time is moving on the other side of the portal. Or maybe it's moving at a much slower pace than it's moving on this side. When I went back last time, it didn't seem like any time had passed while I was gone. It was the same time as it was when I left. Or pretty close to it, anyway."

"So, time is either moving super-fast on this side of the portal or super-slow on the other side of the portal?" Alex asked, working it out in his head.

"Yes. Or maybe it's both. At least, that's what I think," Bill answered. "As far as the question about how we survive until December 26th... I think we take it one day at a time. I don't see that we have a choice. We do the best we can, and in the time between now and then, we figure out a plan for getting back into the mine."

"OK," Thomas said. "Right now, that seems like our only option. But if it is, we have to start thinking about some basics pretty soon. Like, how will we get through the rest of today? We need to find food and shelter before it gets dark. We don't want to be sitting here on a bunch of rocks at midnight."

Mary's brain kicked into action. Until now, she had been completely overwhelmed by the idea that her family had somehow slipped through a time portal. Now that her husband had defined an immediate problem, there were things they could do. They could find food and a place to stay for one night. Those were things that could be managed. She stood up and brushed off her skirt.

"Well, we aren't going to solve that problem by sitting here, are we?"

"No, you're right," Bill said. "We should start walking to the main part of town. While we're doing that, we can talk about our money problem."

"What money problem?" Thomas asked.

"The problem that the money in our pockets is dated more than a hundred and fifty years in the future. And how there's no such thing as a credit card in 1869."

The Taylors shared worried looks.

"Fortunately, I have three small bottles of gold in my shirt pocket that I use for gold panning demonstrations. If I can sell those, we can use the money we get for them."

After a pause, Bill continued, "So, here's what I'm thinking. The International Hotel is going to have all the modern conveniences of the day, like indoor plumbing and gas lighting in each room. They were famous for it. I think we're going to want those conveniences, so we should see if we can get a couple of rooms there. It isn't too far away—just up the hill a few blocks, and at the other end of C Street. For tonight, maybe, Mary, Natalie and Benjamin could share one room, and Thomas, Alex and I could share the other one. What do you think?"

"That sounds fine to me," Thomas said. "You're the only one with any money we can use, and you know a lot more about the town than we do. We'll follow your lead."

"With our thanks for sharing your gold with us," Mary added.

"You're very welcome," Bill said. "We need to stick together while we figure this out, and I'm just glad I have some gold in my pocket."

They started walking up the hill, turning right when they reached D Street. After walking for several more blocks, they came to the intersection of D Street and Taylor Street.

"This seems like a good place to take a quick break," Bill said, "but keep an eye out for runaway wagons. These hills are really steep."

Mary checked to see if any wagons were in sight and slipped a protective arm around Benjamin's shoulders, pulling him a little closer. Natalie used her hat to fan her face and lifted her skirt a few inches to allow some air to circulate around her legs. They all watched for a minute as a woman in a long dress dumped water from a pan into the side yard of a small building, and a man hung up row after row of bedsheets to dry in the sun.

"That must be a Laundry," Bill said, as they started walking again. "There will be several of them in town."

After walking up Taylor Street for a few minutes they reached C Street, but they saw immediately that it would be awhile before they made any further progress towards the International Hotel. A Fourth of July parade had begun, and the C Street boardwalk was packed. They stood at the corner, watching a horse that was pulling a small cannon down the middle of the road. Following the cannon were a marching band and a horse-drawn wagon filled with town dignitaries wearing sashes across their chests.

Everywhere they looked, they saw cheering people. Horses pulled red, white, and blue floats. The floats were followed by groups of marching men holding up signs that said 'Odd Fellows,' 'Sons of Temperance,' 'German Singing Society,' and 'Virginia City Guards.' Spectators shouted greetings to the marchers, who waved and shouted back.

Natalie was trying to take it all in when she spotted a green plaid handkerchief on the ground, just a couple of feet away. She maneuvered closer so she could pick it up.

Tapping the arm of the man standing closest to the handkerchief, she said, "I believe you dropped this, sir."

"I don't know what you're talking about," the man replied, barely looking at her. His voice had an Irish lilt, but he was frowning. "I've never seen that before. Get away from me."

Well, that was rude, she thought, looking around to see if anyone else would claim the handkerchief. After a few minutes, she squeezed back over to her family, still holding the handkerchief. She wasn't sure what to do with it. Nobody appeared to want it, but dropping it back on the ground seemed like littering. She hesitated for a moment before tucking the handkerchief into her father's backpack.

"Head lice?" asked a voice next to her.

Startled, Natalie looked up to see a young woman staring at her head.

"Such a shame you had to cut off your hair," the woman said.

"What?" Natalie asked. Realizing, a moment later, what the woman was thinking, she exclaimed, "I didn't have to cut my hair! I don't have head lice!"

The woman nodded. "Of course you don't," she said, moving away from Natalie as best she could in the crowd.

Natalie turned back to the parade and tried to ignore her, but she could still hear the woman talking.

"Well, she must have head lice. Why else would they would shave her hair off like that?"

A different voice answered, "Just keep your distance, Abbie. You don't want any lice jumping on you!"

The heat rose in Natalie's face. She pulled on the hat she'd been using as a fan and pretended not to hear. When the parade was finally over, she was the first to say, "Let's go!" She didn't even mind when her father insisted everyone hold hands while they walked, so the people by who were pushing their way through the crowd wouldn't separate them. They were making slow progress along C Street when Bill suddenly stopped in his tracks.

"Look! There's an assay office across the street," he exclaimed. "That's perfect! They'll evaluate my gold and turn it into cash. Wait here—I'll be right back!"

He pushed his way into the street and across to the other side. The Taylors continued to take in their surroundings while they waited for him. A steady stream of people moved past them, and they huddled up against the building to avoid the pull of the crowd. As she looked around, Natalie spotted another handkerchief, laying on the ground. It was in the middle of C Street, and it had lacy edges. It was probably white, although it was hard to be sure because it had been stepped on several times. Without a second thought, she pushed her way through the crowd and dashed into the street to retrieve it.

"Natalie!" her mother shouted, "Come back here this instant!"

Natalie scooped up the handkerchief and scurried back, holding her prize.

"I'm sorry, but I saw this handkerchief," she explained.

"Don't you remember what Bill said about watching out for wagons?" Natalie cringed as her mother scolded her. "You didn't even look before you ran out into the street! You could have been killed!"

Natalie hung her head. "I'm sorry, Mom. Really sorry. I'll be more careful from now on."

Since they were still waiting for Bill, Natalie occupied herself by doing what she could to shake the dirt off the handkerchief.

"Do you think it's good luck if you find two handkerchiefs in one day?" she asked Alex.

"No. I think it means people didn't have tissues in 1869," Alex replied. "I'll bet these people drop a hundred handkerchiefs a day."

Natalie put the lacy handkerchief in her father's backpack and settled back against the wall.

"Well, I think it's a sign of good luck," she said.

"I think it's a sign that you're crazy," Alex said. "You don't know what kind of germs there might be on those handkerchiefs."

Natalie's face fell, and she rubbed her hands down the sides of her skirt several times. She wished she had some hand sanitizer.

A few minutes later, Bill returned to the group.

"I was able to sell my gold to the assayer, but there's good news and bad news. First, the bad news.

I only got eighty dollars for my gold. The good news is that things don't cost as much in 1869. It will only be two dollars a night for a room at the International Hotel, so two rooms will only cost us four dollars."

"So, you have enough money to last for several days," Thomas said. "That's a relief."

"Yes, it is," Bill agreed.

They rejoined the crowd that was moving north on C Street, holding hands, trying to stay close together. Finally, with one powerful pull, Bill yanked the entire group through the crowd and into the lobby of the International Hotel.

"Oh, my goodness!" exclaimed Mary, tucking several loose strands of hair back up into her hat. "There are so many people!"

Turning her attention to the children, she used her fingers to wipe a smudge off Benjamin's face and pulled Natalie's hat down further on her head, so nobody could see the shaved sides.

Bill and Thomas went together to the front counter of the hotel to see about securing rooms for the night.

"May I help you?" asked the clerk at the counter, peering at them over the rims of his glasses.

"We'd like to get two rooms, please," Bill replied, "Adjoining rooms, if possible."

"Very good, sir," said the clerk. "The cost is two dollars per night, per room. We do have two adjoining rooms on the third floor. How many nights?"

Bill and Thomas looked at each other. "One night. At least for now," Bill said, handing over the four dollars.

"Thank you," said the clerk, as he opened an enormous book and spun it around so it was facing Bill. They watched in fascination as the clerk dipped a fountain pen into a small bottle of ink before handing the pen to Bill.

"Please sign the register," the clerk said, pointing to a spot on the page. "Right here, next to the lines for Room Numbers 307 and 309."

Bill carefully held the old-fashioned pen. "Sure thing," he said, trying to sound confident. He placed the tip of the pen against the register page and slowly signed his name.

"It's a little blotchy," he said when he finished.

"Quite all right, sir. It happens," the clerk said. "Here are your room keys. Third floor. The stairs are right over there, across the lobby."

It only took a few minutes to find Rooms 307 and 309. As soon as they went inside, Bill opened the door between the rooms so the family could easily travel back and forth. Alex and Natalie stared out the window of Room 309, while everyone else gathered at the window in Room 307.

"This is just unreal," Alex said.

Benjamin said, "I really like the horses! Can we get a horse?"

"Definitely not," said Mary. "We have a lot of other things to figure out before we start thinking about horses."

"That's true," Bill said. "We do have a lot to figure out. But something kind of awesome occurred to me a few minutes ago."

Everyone looked at him expectantly.

"I know where all the gold and silver is going to be found in this county for the next hundred and fifty years!"

Their mouths dropped open and they stared at him with wide eyes. Thomas recovered first.

"Holy smokes!"

"Exactly!" said Bill. "I was thinking, if I can get some help with shoveling dirt, we can stake a few gold mining claims and make a lot of money."

"I could help you," Thomas said. "So could Alex and Natalie."

"I'm sure Natalie could help," Bill replied, "but it was very rare for a woman to do any mining work in the 1800s. People would react badly if they saw her out there with us, digging in the dirt." He looked at Natalie and said, "I'm sure you're very capable, but the three of us guys should really be the ones doing the digging."

"I'm actually OK with that," Natalie said, smiling. Shoveling dirt didn't sound like a lot of fun.

"Since I know exactly where we need to dig, we'll have no trouble finding enough gold to buy whatever we need," Bill continued, "but it's still a lot of hard work digging it up. With three of us digging, though, it shouldn't take very long before we can rent a house in town. In the meantime, we have enough money to stay at the hotel for at least a week, and our claims should be producing by then."

"I have to say, I never thought I would be a gold miner," Thomas said. "But Alex and I will help you any way we can. Right, Alex?"

"Sure!" Alex answered, sounding a little more confident than he felt.

"All right then," Mary said. "This is good! We have a plan. I think the next thing we need to do is find someplace to get dinner. I'm not sure I can eat anything, but I know the children are getting hungry. Especially Alex."

"What about the Star Restaurant?" Bill asked. "We passed it on our way to the hotel."

"Yes!" Alex agreed. "That sounds good. I'm starved. Let's go there."

Mary reached out and pulled him into a hug.

"It's nice to know there are still some things we can count on," she said, kissing the top of his head.

"Can we please go and get something to eat?" Alex asked in a muffled voice.

She released him, and said, "OK. Let's go check out the Star Restaurant."

Chapter 3

Figuring It Out

The bell above the door to the Star Restaurant announced the arrival of the Taylors and Bill. The restaurant was busy, and it looked like there was only one waitress. She had dark brown hair streaked with gray, pulled back into a tidy bun, and she was taking an order from two rough-looking men seated at a table near the front window. Seeing the family come in, she smiled.

"Welcome to the Star Restaurant," she said to them cheerfully. She waved her pencil at the few remaining unoccupied tables in a dark corner at the back. "Just take a seat wherever you can find one, and I'll be right with you."

Weaving their way through the crowded restaurant, they located an unoccupied table that was big enough for all six of them.

"It's really dark back here," Bill said, sitting down. "I wonder if we can get a candle or something."

"Maybe it's supposed to be romantic," Natalie said.

"I don't think this is where people come for a romantic dinner," Bill said. "I'm sure there are much fancier restaurants in town where people go for romance, but this place won't be as expensive as they are."

"And we don't want to judge a book by its cover," her mother added. "The waitress seems nice and everything looks clean. Let's wait and see how the food is."

"Did you see the chalkboard by the door when we came in?" Bill asked. "I think that's probably the entire menu. Small local diners like this aren't necessarily going to have individual menus."

Everyone turned to see what Bill was talking about just as the waitress arrived at their table.

"Hi! I'm Caroline," she said, setting a small kerosene lamp in the center of the table. "I thought you folks could use a little more light back here. Will you be wanting breakfast or dinner?"

"Um, what is dinner?" Thomas asked.

"Today we have pot roast and potatoes," she replied.

"Could I get that with a salad?" Mary asked.

"Oh, no, ma'am," Caroline replied, "We don't have the fixings for a salad. We do have some leftover greens from yesterday, if you'd like those, but it'll be two cents extra if you do."

"No, that's all right," Mary replied. "I don't need to have greens. Thank you, though, for letting me know about them."

"So everybody's going to have dinner?" Caroline asked.

43

Everyone nodded.

"Toast or bread?" she asked.

They all decided on toast, with iced tea or water to drink, except for Bill, who asked for a cup of coffee instead. The service was quick, and it wasn't long before they had finished eating. Caroline came back to give them their check, and Bill asked, "How do you make your coffee? It was delicious!"

"It's the cinnamon I add to it," she said, smiling. "I'm glad you liked it!"

Smiling back at her, Bill said, "I did, and I will definitely come back for more."

"Well, I'll look forward to seeing you, then." Before she left the table, Caroline bent down to whisper in Mary's ear, "If you use vinegar and lard, you won't have to shave the children's heads."

She gave Mary's shoulder a small squeeze and then smiled once more at the entire family. "Come back again, soon!" she said.

Mary blushed, and said, "Put your hat back on, Natalie."

The sun was setting when they left the restaurant, and a cool evening breeze was blowing. The streets were less crowded now, so they decided to take a walk through the town. Ladies with long dresses appeared on the balconies that bordered C Street, chatting with each other as they watched the ongoing Fourth of July festivities. On the streets below, children ran around with sparklers, and men set off firecrackers and roman candles.

The constant noise of the stamp mills crushing rocks from the mines, combined with the popping sounds of the firecrackers and the occasional cheers from the people in the streets, made it hard to talk while they were walking. Eventually, they stopped trying and just watched the holiday activities as they walked. They stopped and looked in the windows of the various stores they passed along the way.

After a couple of hours, the town finally started winding down. Benjamin was so tired he was practically sleepwalking. Thomas lifted him up and put him on his shoulders, while Mary slipped off his sneakers and carried them, so they wouldn't be so conspicuous. When they finally returned to the International Hotel, Benjamin was sound asleep on his father's shoulders. His body was limp, and his cheek was resting on top of Thomas's head.

"What do you think about putting him to bed in one room, and the rest of us gathering in the other room?" Thomas asked. "I'd like to talk about our plans a little more, and I think Alex and Natalie should take part in the conversation."

"Good idea," Mary said.

While she tucked Benjamin into bed in Room 307, everyone else gathered in the next room. When she joined them a few minutes later, she saw that

Thomas and Bill had emptied their pockets onto one of the beds.

Reaching for the backpack, she shook out its contents onto the bed, too. They all stood there, looking at the pile of jumbled items. It was everything they owned in 1869, and it wasn't much.

"Is that a Swiss Army knife?" Alex asked, surveying the pile.

"Yep," Bill answered, picking it up. "It's the deluxe model." One by one, he pulled out the blades and tools tucked into the knife's crevice. "It has a knife, a screwdriver, scissors, a bottle opener, a can opener, a file, a little saw, tweezers, and it even has a toothpick."

"That will probably come in handy," Thomas said, sorting through the things he and Mary had added. "I don't think we have anything nearly as useful. One wallet, two sets of car keys, a few coins, the two handkerchiefs that Nat found today, the vials of gold from your gold-panning demonstration, two parasols, a packet of tissues, and the clothes we were wearing this morning, when we were back in our own time. That's it."

"It's not a lot," Bill observed, picking up his watch and noting that it was still frozen in time, "but we also have the money from the gold I took to the assayer. We'll be OK. We'll make it work."

"There is something else that I've been thinking about," Thomas said. "Maybe it goes without saying, but I think it's important we make it clear to the children—we can't go around talking about how we came here from the future. Are we all in agreement about that?"

"Definitely," Bill replied. "If we tell the truth, people will think we're crazy, and in this century that will get you a one-way ticket to an asylum. If we're locked up, we'll never get back to our own time."

"That's an excellent point," Mary said. "Obviously, we can't tell people the truth. Nobody would believe us, anyway. We're going to have to be careful about what we say." Looking directly at Alex and Natalie, she continued. "Actually, it isn't just about keeping quiet. We need to get our story straight, and then we have to stick to it—and we'll all have to watch Ben pretty carefully for a while."

Alex and Natalie both nodded their heads.

"And Natalie, you know we have to do something about your hair, right?"

"Oh, yeah, I know," Natalie replied. "Those ladies at the parade were awful."

Alex smiled broadly and said, "I thought it was hilarious!"

Natalie glared at him for a second and then decided her brother's teasing was a small thing that didn't need to be worried about right now.

"We understand what you're saying, Mom," she said. "We totally get it. So when people ask us where we're from, what's our story?"

47

"I think we should say we came from San Francisco," Bill suggested. "That's the nearest big city, and in 1869, that's where most of Virginia City's supplies came from. People are used to seeing all kinds of strange things delivered from San Francisco, so it'll be a good cover story."

"Another thing we should think about," Thomas said, "is maybe we should start calling Mr. Johnson 'Uncle Bill.' We need to stick together and people will think it's odd if we don't seem to be related to each other."

"That's a good idea," Mary said.

"I agree," Bill said, "that's an excellent idea."

Looking over at Alex and Natalie, Mary said, "You got that, right? Meet your new Uncle Bill."

"Hi, Uncle Bill," said Alex.

"Hi, Uncle Bill," said Natalie, reaching out and shaking Bill's hand.

"It would be good if we knew more about you, Uncle Bill," Mary said. "Are you from Virginia City? Do you have family here?"

"I'm not originally from Virginia City," Bill replied, "but once I discovered it, that's where I wanted to be. I had a career in the Army, and when I retired, my wife and I settled down here. She passed away a few years ago, and I've been on my own, ever since."

"Oh, I'm so sorry to hear about your wife," Mary said. "Do you have any children?"

"No, we never had any children, but Becky and I had a grand time together. We traveled the world and had all kinds of adventures. Thinking about her makes me smile. I like to think she's smiling down on me, too—or maybe laughing at me, sometimes," he said, shaking his head.

After a pause, he continued, "Anyway, I've been gold prospecting and gold mining whenever I could, since I was eight years old. I have a knack for it, and I'm a pretty good teacher, too—which brings me to our plans for tomorrow." Turning to Thomas, he said, "I'd like to get started prospecting first thing in the morning, if you and Alex are up for it. We need to start making money as soon as we can."

"I agree," Thomas said. "We're ready, right Alex?"

"Right!" Alex responded.

"All right then," Bill said, "Tomorrow morning we'll need to pack a lunch and take something to drink. The place I'm thinking of, where we'll stake our claims, is called Gold Canyon. It's about two miles from here. We'll be gone for the better part of the day. On our way there we'll buy some of the gold mining equipment we need, so we can test the dirt and make sure we're in a good spot. We won't need all of our cash for that, so I'll leave the rest of it with you, Mary. That way you'll can pay for food, or anything else you need, while we're gone."

"Thank you," Mary said. "What do you think about using the backpack to carry your lunches?"

"Good idea," Bill said. "That'll be one less thing we have to buy."

"Will you be OK here by yourself all day with Natalie and Ben?" Thomas asked her.

"We'll be fine," Mary replied. "Don't worry about us. We'll explore the town a little more and look for a pair of shoes for Ben. His sneakers look very out of place in 1869."

"It's settled then," Bill said. "When we head out in the morning, I'll stop by the front desk and pay for three more days here at the hotel. That should give us plenty of time to find some gold and restock our supply of cash."

"Thank you, again," Mary said. "You're becoming a very good friend, very quickly."

"Aw, shucks," Bill said. "Ask Thomas and Alex if they agree with you after they've been shoveling dirt with me all day!"

Everybody laughed, and some of the tension they had been feeling eased a little bit.

"Well, I think the best thing we can do now is try to get some sleep," Thomas said. "Today has been very eventful—to say the least! And tomorrow is going to be another big day."

Mary nodded in agreement.

Bill said, "I could definitely use some sleep."

Mary and Natalie picked up their belongings and carried them into Room 307, where Benjamin was already sleeping. In the bathroom sink, Mary carefully washed their clothes and the handkerchiefs Natalie had found, and hung everything up to dry. Shortly after that, they were all in bed.

Bill went right to sleep, and Benjamin had been sound asleep for a couple of hours, but the rest of the Taylor family had a harder time drifting off. An hour later, Alex was wondering what, exactly, the lumpy mattress was made of, and whether he would get any sleep at all. His father had opened the window as far as it would go, but the room still seemed hot and stuffy.

He tried to lie still, and quiet his mind. Then he calculated the number of days until December 26th. Five months and twenty-two days. One hundred and seventy-five days. Either way, it sounded like a very long time. Instead of drifting off to sleep, he lay awake for another two hours, thinking about the reality of 175 days, and the peculiar lump in the mattress right below his shoulders. He finally drifted off, but it seemed like he had only been asleep for a few minutes when he woke up to the sound of loud snoring.

Peering out from under the covers, he squinted against the sunlight that was streaming in through the window.

51

"Dad, you're snoring—really loud," he said to the lump under the covers of the bed next to him.

"What? No, I'm not," said his father's voice behind him.

Alex rolled over in surprise and then remembered that he and his father had shared one of the beds last night.

"Oh, sorry. It's Mr. Johnson. I mean, Uncle Bill. I thought it was you that was snoring, Dad. I guess this means yesterday wasn't a dream. We really are here, in 1869?"

"Yes, we really are," Thomas replied. "It's 1869. This is for real."

Groaning, Alex rolled onto his back and stared at the ceiling for a moment. "Well, I hope Uncle Bill doesn't snore like that all the time."

In the room next door, Natalie was also staring at the ceiling. She hadn't slept much the night before, either. Her mattress was just as lumpy as the one Alex had, but she lay perfectly still, not wanting to disturb her mother. Benjamin was sound asleep, and he looked very comfortable in the bed he wasn't sharing with anyone. He hadn't spent the night worrying about anything. Natalie stared at him for a while with envy.

Lying there quietly, she didn't know that her mother was also wide awake, making a mental list of everything they would need to set up a home. Pots, pans, plates, forks, spoons, blankets—the list went on, and she tried to estimate the cost. She kept thinking about their belongings, dumped on the bed the night before. It was such a small pile. They were practically starting with nothing. Not wanting to disturb her daughter, Mary lay still on the bed and quietly worried. Would Bill be able to find gold quickly? Should she try to find a job in town? Could Natalie take care of Benjamin if she got a job? Eventually, she set those thoughts aside and decided to concentrate on getting through one day at a time. Taking a deep breath, she rolled out of the bed.

"OK, kiddos," she said, "It's time to get up. We have things to do, and we're burning daylight!"

As soon as everyone was awake and dressed, they headed back to the Star Restaurant for breakfast. To their surprise, Caroline was once again their waitress.

"Don't you ever go home?" Bill asked her.

"Yes, of course I do!" she said, laughing. "I was filling in for Annabeth yesterday evening. I usually only work the breakfast and lunch shifts."

"Well, it's nice to see you again." Bill took a sip of his cinnamon-flavored coffee. "And I sure do like your coffee."

After they finished breakfast, Bill, Thomas, and Alex were ready to start their day of prospecting in Gold Canyon. Mary, Natalie, and Benjamin watched them for a while as they walked south on C Street, then they turned and headed back to the hotel.

"I saw Beck's Hardware Store last night, at the corner of C Street and Taylor Street," Bill said, as he, Thomas, and Alex continued walking through the town. "We can stop there to get the shovels and gold pans we'll need today. They probably have the rocker box we need, too, but that can wait for another day."

They reached the hardware store just a few minutes later, and Alex was the first one through the door.

"Whoa!" he exclaimed, as he looked around. "This place is amazing!"

Every inch of the store was crammed full of tools and equipment. Alex could see an array of hammers, screwdrivers, saws, nails, screws, coffeepots, frying pans, picks, shovels, and gold pans made of tin.

"It looks like they have a good selection of gold panning equipment in that corner over there," Bill said. "When we come back tomorrow, we'll get that rocker box. For today we just need three shovels, two pickaxes, and three gold pans."

"What's a rocker box?" asked Alex.

"See that thing that looks kind of like a baby cradle?" Bill asked, pointing to a small wooden contraption in the corner. "You shovel dirt into that box at the top, and rock it side to side. Big rocks get stuck in the box at the top, and everything else goes down through the part that's sticking out in the front. That's the chute. It collects the heavier dirt and gold. Then you take out the dirt that collected in the chute and you pan it out."

Bill selected three shovels, and handed them to Thomas. "And that, my friends, is called placer gold mining. It's spelled like 'place-er', but it sounds like 'plasser'. It just means that you get the gold out of the dirt, instead of breaking rocks apart to find it."

He led them to a display of pickaxes and selected two, hefting them up onto his shoulder.

"Alex, if you'll grab twelve of those wooden posts, I'll get the gold pans, and we should be all set for today."

After selecting three gold pans, he headed to the front counter to pay for their purchases. Thomas and Alex followed close behind.

"We'll need a piece of charcoal, or something, to mark our claim boundaries," Bill told the cashier.

"I have just the thing," the man replied. "A charcoal pencil. It'll cost you two cents."

"Perfect. We'll take it," Bill said, piling all the items they had collected on the counter.

The clerk motioned to a small box that was sitting open on the counter near the register. "Do you want any of those little drawstring bags? They're on sale."

"Good idea," Bill said, grabbing a handful of them from the box.

After completing their purchase, they headed for the door.

"Good luck!" the cashier called out, putting Bill's money into the cash register.

"Thanks!" Bill called back to him, closing the door behind them. Turning to Thomas and Alex, he quietly added, "But we aren't really going to need a lot of luck, since we know exactly where to go."

Back at the hotel, Natalie and her mother were planning their day, and doing their best to ignore Benjamin, who was pacing back and forth, saying, "I'm bored, I'm bored," over and over again.

"I've been thinking," Mary said. "We should take some time to check out the stores around here while we're looking for shoes for Benjamin. That way we'll know what things are likely to cost when we move out of the hotel."

Before Natalie had a chance to respond, they both noticed the door to their room swinging open. Turning in that direction, they caught a glimpse of Benjamin slipping out of the room and into the long hallway leading to the stairs.

Natalie reacted first. "Benjamin! Stop!" she shouted, running after him with her skirt hiked up around her knees. Although she was running as fast as she could, somehow Benjamin was quicker. She watched as he reached the staircase and climbed up onto the banister that topped the stair railing.

Terrified that he would fall to the first floor below, Natalie stopped running and stood perfectly still. Mary was only a few steps behind her, and she came to a sudden stop, too. Not wanting to startle her son, she caught her breath and whispered, "Benjamin!"

"Come and catch me!" Benjamin called out, giving himself a mighty push, "I'm sliding!"

He picked up speed as slid down the long banister, and was moving very quickly when he reached the second floor landing. Then he slammed into the ornate knob at the bottom of the banister. With a shocked look on his face, he slid off the railing like melting butter.

Natalie raced down the stairs after him, and Mary followed close behind.

"Are you all right?" they both asked when they caught up to him.

"That really hurt," Benjamin said, bursting into tears.

Natalie reached for his hand, feeling the stares of the people in the lobby.

"I'm sorry you hurt yourself, but it kind of serves you right."

Benjamin pulled his hand back and glared at his sister through his tears.

"Come on!" she whispered fiercely, grabbing for her brother's hand. "We have to go back to our room!"

Benjamin was sure he was in trouble with his mother, and he was upset with his sister—plus, his backside was still smarting from his crash landing. He pulled his hand away. "I don't want to go back to that stinky old room! I'm tired of that room. I want to see a cowboy! And I want to play my video games!"

Natalie and Mary exchanged glances and then looked towards the lobby. Several people were watching Benjamin's dramatic performance. Mary silently held her hand out, but Benjamin crossed his arms and stared at the floor. After a few seconds he looked up at her, contrite.

"I'm sorry, Mom," he said, uncrossing his arms and taking her hand.

"I know."

She led him up the stairs, and Natalie followed. When they reached their room, she closed the door firmly, standing for a moment with her head resting against the door. Then she turned to face Benjamin.

"We are going shopping in a few minutes," she told him, "but first, we need to talk about the rules."

"I know the rules," Benjamin assured her, wiping his nose with the palm of his hand. "And there's probably a new rule about not sliding down the stairs, right?"

"Yes," Mary replied, "that is definitely one of the new rules, but there are a few other rules we need to discuss, because we are going to be staying here in Virginia City for a while. Probably for the whole summer, and for Halloween, and Thanksgiving, and Christmas."

"I thought we were going to go home in two weeks," Benjamin said, with a concerned look on his face.

"Well, things have changed," Mary said calmly. "And things are a little different here, so it's very important that you mind your manners, OK?"

Benjamin was puzzled, but he nodded his head. "What's different here?"

"Well, for starters, there are no screens here," Mary said.

"You mean they don't have video games here, or tablets?" Benjamin asked.

"No screens at all. Nothing electronic. And you shouldn't ask about those things, because nobody here will know what you're talking about," Mary answered.

"What about TV?"

"No TV, either. Absolutely no screens. But there are a lot of books, and I'm sure there's a library in town."

Benjamin thought about that for a minute, and said, "OK, I guess we could go to the library, but I'd rather get a horse. I wouldn't miss screens very much if I had a horse."

"I'm sure that's true," Mary said. "But a horse is a big commitment. We can talk about it some more after we've been here for a while."

"That would be so cool!" Benjamin said. "I would help you take care of it."

"I would count on that," Mary replied. "For now, though, I just need you to focus on behaving yourself. Do you understand? This is important. Are you ready to behave like a gentleman?"

"Yes, ma'am," Benjamin said, nodding his head, "I can be a gentleman."

Mary smiled and looked at Natalie. "Well, then, that's settled. We'll all be on our best behavior."

"Right!" said Benjamin.

"Right!" said Natalie, suddenly feeling older than her years. Benjamin's joy ride had made it clear she would have to help her parents keep an eye on her little brother. The simplest things could create huge problems for them, and Benjamin didn't understand that at all.

Squaring her shoulders, she took her brother by the hand, and said, "Hold my hand, and we'll go downstairs together."

Mary smiled gratefully at her daughter. "That's a good idea! I'll be right behind you. I just need to lock the door."

When she reached the staircase, Mary paused and watched her daughter and youngest son walking hand-in-hand down the steps. Benjamin seemed so young, and Natalie suddenly seemed so much older. She hurried down the stairs to catch up with them. *Day two in 1869*, she said to herself. *We can do this.*

That evening, after another dinner at the Star Restaurant, the family gathered on the balcony outside their hotel rooms. The sun was slipping behind Mount Davidson, and Bill had collected six wooden folding chairs from various parts of the hotel, placing them in a circle just outside the balcony door. For a while, they all sat quietly. Even Benjamin, wearing his new leather shoes, was quiet as he played with a small wooden horse Mary had purchased for him earlier that day. After a few minutes, Bill broke the silence.

"We had a good start today," he said, speaking quietly, to avoid drawing the attention of any hotel guests who might be on a nearby balcony. "We started working the claim this afternoon, and there was color in the very first pan. We should be able to find a lot more as we follow the path of the gold."

"How did Alex do today?" Mary asked.

Thomas put his hand on Alex's shoulder. "He did really well," he said, "but I imagine we'll both be a little sore tomorrow from all that shoveling. It turns out that gold mining is quite a workout! Right, Alex?"

Alex nodded his head. He was too tired to talk. All he really wanted was to crawl into bed.

"Poor thing," Mary said, "I know it's hard, but you're being a huge help to Uncle Bill and Dad, and it's just for a couple of months. Once school starts in September you won't have to help them, anymore."

Natalie looked up at her mother. "Until school starts?" she asked. "Are you kidding? We have to go to school here?"

"Well, of course, you have to go to school," Mary replied. "If you don't go to school for six months, your academic skills will slip a lot. Reading, writing, and arithmetic are important, no matter what year it is."

Natalie's head swung back and forth as she looked at her parents in disbelief. When she saw they were serious, she slumped down in her chair.

"I think you'll be looking forward to school by the time September rolls around," Mary said. "Just wait and see."

"And you'll have a chance to make new friends," Bill offered optimistically.

Going to school actually sounded good to Alex at that moment, so he nodded his head in agreement.

"Traitor!" Natalie said.

"Mmm," Alex replied, with his eyes shut. It was the best he could do.

Before long, Alex was asleep in his chair, oblivious to the muted conversation that continued around him for the next couple of hours.

The temperature dropped several degrees after the sun had set, and a steady breeze made it a very pleasant evening to be sitting outdoors.

Eventually, Benjamin fell asleep in his chair, too, leaving Natalie alone to listen to the adults talking about the price of gold, the cost of living, and the possibility of renting a vacant house on B Street.

"I saw a sign on the front porch that says it has three bedrooms and it's fully furnished, so we wouldn't have to buy very much furniture. It has a backyard, too," Mary said. "They're asking $16 a month, which is much less than what we're paying here at the hotel."

"That sounds good," Bill said. "Can you check to see if they'll rent it to us?"

"Yes, I'll do that tomorrow. Let's keep our fingers crossed," she said, stifling a yawn. "It would be great if it worked out."

Thomas looked over at his sleeping sons. "The house sounds good," he said, "but right now, I'm really tired. I'm going to take a cue from these two sleepyheads and call it a night."

"Me, too," Bill agreed. "We need to get up early and get to over the courthouse as soon as it opens, so we can register our claims."

Mary roused Alex and Benjamin enough to move them towards their beds. In less than fifteen minutes, they were all sound asleep, and unlike the night before, everyone slept soundly through the night.

Chapter 4

Things Are Looking Up

Early the next morning, Bill, Thomas, and Alex set out for the county courthouse. They got there twenty minutes before the Recorder's Office opened, but there was already a long line winding down two flights of stairs and out the front door.

Yesterday they had pounded wooden stakes into the ground to mark the boundaries of their claims, and now they needed to have them officially documented. Promptly at 8:00, the doors to the office opened, and the line started moving. At 10:00 they finally found themselves at the front of the line.

While they waited to be called into the office, Alex shifted his weight from one leg to the other and picked at the blisters on his hands. He wondered what his sister and brother were doing back at the hotel. Whatever it was, he figured it had to be more fun than standing in line or shoveling dirt.

A few minutes later, the man that had been in front of them left the Recorder's Office. A voice from inside the room called out, "Next!" and Bill, Thomas, and Alex finally entered the office. A man stood at a cashier's window behind a long counter. In front of him was an open ledger book. A nameplate to the man's right identified him as D. B. Rawlson.

"Yes?" he asked.

"We'd like to record three claims," Bill said.

"As a group or separately?"

"As a group," Thomas said.

Mr. Rawlson turned to a fresh page in the book, dipped his pen into an inkwell, and wrote, "We the undersigned claim for mining purposes 200 feet each, three claims." He looked up and said, "Describe the location."

"It's the Gold Canyon creek bed, running up the creek 600 feet, on the east side of Grizzly Hill," Bill said.

Returning to his ledger book, Mr. Rawlson wrote "on the Gold Canyon creek bed, running up the creek 600 feet, east of Grizzly Hill, 200 feet by 600 feet."

"What are your names?" he asked.

"William Johnson, Thomas Taylor, and Alexander Taylor."

When he finished writing their names, he spun the book around.

"Sign here."

When they finished signing, Mr. Rawlson spun the book around once more and wrote "Filed for Record, July 6, 1869." He signed it with a flourish, then looked up, and said, "That'll be seventy-five cents."

Bill handed him the money, while Alex rubbed at the ink smudges on his fingers.

Thomas asked, "Is that it?"

"Yes," Mr. Rawlson replied. "That's it. Next!"

Thomas and Alex looked at each other in surprise.

"Well, that part was easy," Bill said.

They made their way down the stairs and past the long line of people still waiting to file their claims. Once they were outside, they headed back to the hotel to pick up the mining equipment they had purchased the day before. With their picks, shovels, and gold pans in hand, they set out for Beck's Hardware, where they bought a rocker box and a small wagon they could use to haul everything. After one more stop to pick up sandwiches, they set out for their claim. In high spirits, they walked briskly through the town. They were in a hurry to start mining gold, and there were still several good hours of daylight left.

Back at the hotel, Mary was doing her best to straighten Natalie's naturally curly hair, so it would cover the shaved sides of her head. Two more people had mentioned head lice while they were shopping the day before, which had infuriated Natalie and embarrassed Mary. If they were going to have any luck renting a house, Mary thought it would be best if the property owner didn't have reason to think their daughter had lice.

"I'm sorry. I know you hate this, but maybe if we part it in the middle, and then pull it into a ponytail..." her voice trailed off as she tugged on Natalie's hair.

"Ouch!" Natalie yelped, while Mary struggled to tie her daughter's curly hair back with the white handkerchief she had retrieved from the middle of C Street two days earlier. Now that it was clean, it was very pretty, with delicate lace sewn around its edges.

"There!" Mary exclaimed, "Got it!"

She stepped back to get a better look, squinting a little, and cocking her head to one side. "Well, you can't really see the shaved parts anymore."

Natalie got up from her chair and checked out her reflection in the mirror above the chest of drawers.

"Mom! That looks.... terrible!" Natalie said. "It's flat and fuzzy at the same time."

"I know it's not your best look, but it's better than everybody thinking you have head lice. It's either this, or you wear a hat all the time."

Natalie frowned. "These people are stupid," she said, talking to her mother's reflection in the mirror.

"No, they aren't stupid," Mary corrected her, "they live in a different time, when girls never shaved their heads. The only explanation they can think of is that you had a bad case of lice. We have to remember that things are different in 1869."

"Oh, I don't think I'll need much reminding with my hair pulled so tight."

Mary gave Natalie a quick hug and then turned her attention to Benjamin.

"How about you, young man?" she asked. "Let me see your face. Did you brush your teeth this morning?"

"Yes, but that tooth powder is disgusting," he said. "Why can't we use regular toothpaste?"

"Because they don't have toothpaste here," his mother replied. "We talked about that, remember? We all have to use toothpowder right now. Try putting a little water on it before you brush your teeth. That makes it more like a paste. I'm sorry, buddy, but I'm very glad you brushed your teeth without anybody telling you to. Nice job!"

"It was gross," he said, "I hate the bristles. I don't like the way the handle feels, either, but I did it."

"Well, thank you," Mary said. "I'm glad you have clean teeth. Are we all ready to go now? I want to ask about the rental house on B Street this morning before someone else gets it."

"Ready," Natalie said.

"Ready!" Benjamin exclaimed, with much more enthusiasm than Natalie had shown.

"All right," Mary said, opening the hotel room door. "Here we go! Everybody cross your fingers, and look respectable."

Much later that day, as the sun was setting, the door to the hotel room flew open and Alex came rushing in. Mary, Natalie, and Benjamin all jumped, startled by his sudden entrance.

"You won't believe it!" he exclaimed.

"Won't believe what? Where is your father? Where is Uncle Bill?"

"They're right behind me," Alex said. "I was too excited to walk with them, so I ran."

"Excited about what?" Mary asked.

"Gold!" Alex said in a loud whisper. "Uncle Bill told me to keep it quiet, but we did really well today. Our claims are full of gold!"

Mary jumped up from her chair and gave Alex a hug.

"That's wonderful news!" she said, as Thomas and Bill came in through the open door. "Alex was just telling us your news!"

Bill carefully shut the door, and said, "It's true. Our claims are in a sweet spot. We just have to keep it quiet so we don't attract claim jumpers."

"What's a claim jumper?" Benjamin asked.

"That's somebody who comes and steals gold from your claim when you aren't there. Usually, that happens when bad people find out a particular claim has a lot of gold, so we need to keep it a secret. We don't want anyone to know how rich our claim is, because we don't anybody to steal from us."

"So what's the plan?" Mary asked. "You'll need to take the gold to the assayer's office. Won't the assayer tell people about it?"

"Here's what I'm thinking," Bill said, taking off his hat and running his hand over his head. "We'll save the bigger nuggets by putting them somewhere safe, and we'll take the smaller pieces of gold to the assayer. When our claim is played out, and we're ready to move on to a new claim, that's when we'll take the nuggets to him. That way, we'll already have all the gold from that claim and there won't be anything left for anyone to steal from us."

"OK," Mary said, "But how much are the smaller pieces of gold worth? Is it enough to pay the rent on the house we were talking about? Because I have exciting news, too!"

Instead of answering, Bill turned to Thomas and said, "You should show her the small gold we found today."

With a smile, Thomas reached into his shirt pocket and pulled out one of the small drawstring bags they had purchased the day before. He loosened the string and walked over to the dresser, where he carefully poured the contents of the bag onto its polished surface.

When he finished pouring, Mary, Natalie and Benjamin stared at the small pile of gold in silence.

"Not counting the nuggets, which will be our secret," Bill said, "what you see right there is about $50 worth of gold."

"Really? That's wonderful!" Mary exclaimed. "Because Mr. French, the man who owns the rental house, said he would hold the house for us until noon tomorrow. I think we should go see him right now and pay him the first month's rent! He gave me his address," she said, rushing over to the bedside table where she had put Mr. French's business card. "See? Here it is on the back of his card."

"Excellent!" Bill said, reading the address on the back of the card. "Thomas and I will head over to the assayer's office to trade this gold for cash. Then we'll meet you at Mr. French's house in about twenty minutes, OK?"

"Sounds perfect!" Mary said, walking with the two men to the hotel room door. "We'll see you there in twenty minutes!"

After she closed the door, Mary turned to her children and smiled. "Things are starting to look up! I'm so proud of you, Alex. Thank you. I know mining is hard work."

"I think my blisters have blisters," Alex said, "but it's worth it when you see all that gold in your pan." He turned, and for the first time noticed his sister's new hairstyle. "Holy moly!" he said, "You look, uh, very strange with your hair like that."

"You know what, Alex?" Natalie responded, "I don't really care what you think."

"Oh," Alex said. It wouldn't be much fun if his sister wasn't going to react to his teasing. He tried again.

"I was just surprised. I guess you took care of that pesky head lice problem, huh?"

"You don't know when to quit, do you, Barf Brain?"

"There she is!" Alex said, smiling. "That's the sister I know and love."

He ducked to avoid the pillow she threw at him.

"Head lice," he said again, dodging another pillow.

"All right, knock it off," Mary said. "You're going to break something if you keep throwing pillows around. Alex, please stop teasing your sister. Go wash up, and then we'll head over to Mr. French's house."

"Yes, ma'am," Alex said, heading for the doorway that separated the two rooms. As soon as he was out of sight, he started singing a song he had just made up, to the tune of "Mary Had a Little Lamb."

"My sister don't have head lice, have head lice, have head lice."

Natalie scowled in his direction.

"Brothers!" she said, shaking her head in disgust.

Chapter 5

Moving In

The Taylor family moved into their new house as soon as they signed the rental agreement with Mr. French. It had been a very easy move since they didn't own anything except their clothes, some gold mining equipment, and the few items they had piled on the hotel bed during their first night in 1869. Alex, Natalie, and Benjamin were sharing the biggest bedroom in the house, and Uncle Bill had taken the smallest bedroom, leaving Thomas and Mary with the middle-sized bedroom. They were all enjoying the extra space, but it was much noisier at the house than it had been at the hotel. They were closer to the stamp mills now, and they could hear the rocks from the mines being crushed and pounded twenty-four hours a day.

For the first couple of nights, nobody slept very well, but by the third night they were all getting used to the constant crashing and banging sounds, along with the hissing noises from the pumps that drained water from the mineshafts.

"How did everybody sleep?" Mary asked after their third night in the house. The whole family had straggled into the kitchen where a big wooden dining table with eight chairs was located.

"I'm still wishing the six o'clock whistle was at eight o'clock," Alex said, "but that's not my biggest problem. Can we please get another bed soon? It's killing me to sleep in the same bed with Ben. It's so narrow, and he's so fidgety!"

"I'll see what I can do about getting another bed today," Mary replied. "Although it's going to be pretty cramped in that room once we put in a third bed."

"Are we going out for breakfast?" Natalie asked.

"Yes," Mary sighed. "I'm still getting the hang of the wood-burning stove."

"That's fine with me," Bill said. "We can keep eating at the Star Restaurant for as long as you want."

"Is it the food or the waitress that you like the most?" Alex asked.

Blushing, Bill said "It's both! I like the food, and I like Caroline, too. There's nothing wrong with that."

"She does seem very nice," Mary said.

"Yes, she does," Thomas said.

"Exactly!" Bill said. "I think so, too."

Alex smiled and leaned against the back of his chair.

"So, is everybody ready to get some breakfast?" Bill asked. "I don't know about you guys, but I'm anxious to get back to the claim today."

"I just need a minute," Thomas said. He stuffed both of the handkerchiefs Natalie had found into his pants pocket and sat down to put his boots on. "I'm going to dip a handkerchief in the creek this afternoon and tie it around my neck," he said. "That should help cool me off. If either of you wants to use the other one, it's all yours."

"Good idea," Bill said, "I'll take you up on that offer."

Alex said, "Hello? Could we maybe buy a handkerchief for me, too, at the dry goods store, on our way to the claim? Like, a regular guy's handkerchief?"

"Oh, I guess we could," Bill replied, smiling. "But you won't be as pretty as your dad will be when he's wearing the lacy white handkerchief."

"Actually," Thomas said, handing the lacy white handkerchief to Bill with an even bigger smile, "that one is for you."

Mary jumped into the conversation, and said, "How about if you guys buy yourselves several handkerchiefs this morning, and you leave the pretty white one with me?"

"Well, if you insist," Bill said, pretending to be reluctant as he placed the lacy white handkerchief in Mary's outstretched hand. "I guess I could part with it."

With the matter of handkerchiefs settled, they all headed out the door and walked down the street to the Star Restaurant for breakfast.

As soon as they stepped through the restaurant door, Bill called out to Caroline that he was there for "the best cup of coffee in the world." She was across the room, taking an order, but she looked up and gave him a smile. She watched the family as they headed to their usual table, and then turned her attention back to her customer.

"I'm pretty sure the sparks are flying both ways," Mary said quietly to her husband.

"It does look like that, doesn't it?" Thomas said, with a smile.

They all had a busy day ahead, so when breakfast was over, they parted ways on the boardwalk in front of the restaurant. Bill, Thomas, and Alex headed for their claim, while Mary, Natalie, and Benjamin planned to go to Kearney's Family Groceries & Vegetables, and the LaFayette Meat Market, to buy groceries and some wood for their stove. Mary was determined to figure out how to use the stove in their new house. She wanted to take another shot at it while it was still cool outside, before the sun had a chance to make the house even hotter.

By the time they finished shopping, Mary needed help from both Natalie and Benjamin to carry their purchases home from the market. Benjamin carried a bundle of wood for the stove, while Natalie carried two dozen eggs, a half-pound of bacon, a loaf of bread, and a quarter-pound of butter in a straw basket lined with a red- and green-checked cloth. Mary was carrying a new cast-iron skillet, a metal spatula, a big spoon, and a toasting rack that made toast by holding slices of bread near the fire. Slung over her shoulder was a burlap bag that contained six plates, six mugs, and six sets of silverware. The bag made clanking noises with every step she took, but they could barely hear it over the noise of the mining equipment that was constantly running nearby.

When they got back to the house, Mary built a small fire inside the stove, and then closed the heavy iron door shut. Over the next few minutes, she checked the stove by carefully touching the top, waiting for it to get hot enough to cook on. When it didn't seem to be warming up very much, she added more wood and waited a little longer. Finally, the stove seemed hot enough, and she set the cast-iron skillet on top, filling it with slices of bacon.

Mary, Natalie and Benjamin stood there watching the bacon to see what would happen. At first it was hard to tell if the bacon was cooking at all, but after a minute or so, it started sizzling around the edges.

Using the metal spatula, Mary nudged the bacon around in the pan as it cooked, and then flipped it over to cook on the other side. The fire blazed away inside the oven, and the stovetop started getting hotter and hotter. Soon, the bacon started to burn and Mary rushed to save it. She managed to get three strips onto a plate before smoke was billowing out of the pan.

"Oh, no, no, no!" she exclaimed, reaching to take the pan off the stove. "Ouch! Hot!" she yelped.

Grabbing a dishtowel to use as a potholder, she tried again.

"Open the door!" she shouted to her children.

Natalie ran to the front door and flung it open. Mary ran from the kitchen with the smoking pan and hurried down the front porch steps. With a small grunt of effort, she tossed the entire pan and its contents into the street.

She stood there for a moment staring at the smoking mess, absent-mindedly folding the dishtowel. Then she looked left and right, up and down the street, wondering how many people had witnessed her small disaster.

To her surprise, everybody was carrying on as though nothing unusual was happening in front of the Taylor house. Apparently, a pan full of burning bacon being thrown into the street wasn't particularly interesting to the residents of Virginia City.

Well, thank goodness for that, she thought, as she retrieved the pan from the dirt. Carrying it in her outstretched arm so it wouldn't smudge her dress, she marched back into the house.

"Let's try that again," she said.

Natalie looked at her mother with apprehension. "Are you sure? You know, Bill said he thought it would be fine if we kept eating at the Star Restaurant for a while."

"I'm sure," Mary said, with determination. "I just need some practice. I'll wait for the stove to cool down a little and try it again."

Seeing the looks on her children's faces, she said, "Natalie, why don't you take your brother and go explore the town? Maybe by the time you come back for lunch, I'll have the stove all figured out, and we can have fried eggs and bacon for lunch. OK?"

"Sure, Mom," Natalie said, reaching for her little brother's hand. "Come on, Benjamin. Let's go exploring."

They went out the front door and stepped carefully around the burnt bacon as they crossed the street. Several scrawny-looking dogs were headed towards them, lured by the smell. Benjamin was excited to see them coming, but Natalie pulled him away.

"They could have rabies, or mange, or something," she said.

"That's OK," Benjamin said, "I just want to pet them."

"No, you don't," Natalie assured him. "It would be really bad if a sick dog bit you."

She pulled Benjamin behind her and hurried away from the gathering pack of dogs. He broke into a trot, trying to keep up with her while he considered the possibility that a dog might bite him.

"I would be very careful," he said, after a few minutes, but Natalie didn't hear him, and pretty soon they were both distracted by a pond they could see in the distance.

That evening, everyone had exciting news to share. Bill, Thomas and Alex were tired, but thrilled with the three ounces of small gold and four little nuggets they had found. Bill estimated that the total worth of that day's gold was about $90.

Mary was happy to report that she had finally mastered the wood stove enough to make fried eggs and bacon for lunch.

"My next challenge," she said, "is to figure out how to bake things in a wood-burning oven. I'll start working on that in the next day or two."

Natalie and Benjamin had news, too. They were excited to tell everyone about the pond they had found just below E Street.

"We met a brother and sister named Hannah and John while we were there," Natalie said. "They said it's called the C & C pond, and everybody swims there."

"And there was another boy that was my age," Benjamin chimed in. "His name is Yancy. He has yellow hair, and he only has four toes on one of his feet. His little toe is missing."

"What happened to it?" Alex asked.

"I don't know," Benjamin replied, "I asked him what happened to it, but he didn't tell me."

"That's weird," Alex said. He pondered Yancy's missing toe for a minute, but Natalie interrupted his thoughts.

"Oh! Speaking of weird, you should see the girls' bathing suits here!" she said. "They wear dresses that go down to their knees and really ugly bloomer pants underneath the dress. That's what they wear when they're swimming! It must weigh a ton when it's wet." Turning to her parents, she asked, "Do I have to wear the same thing when I go swimming?"

"Well, yes," Mary replied. "I'm sorry, but if that's what the girls are wearing here, that's what you have to wear, too."

"That's really not fair," Natalie said. "The boys get to wear shorts when they swim."

"I agree that it's not fair," Mary said, "but you still have to wear what the other girls wear if you want to swim. It's important that we blend in, as best we can."

"Your mother's right," Thomas said, "but I'd like to take a look at that pond before any of you go swimming in it. Understood?"

All three of the children nodded.

"We're glad you're making friends," Mary said. "Maybe we can all take a walk and check out the pond after dinner."

"When are we having dinner?" Alex asked. "I'm starved!"

"Of course you are," Mary said with a smile. "What do you guys think about trying a different restaurant for dinner tonight?"

"Sounds good to me," Bill said, "but I think I'll keep going to the Star Restaurant for my breakfast."

"Of course," Mary said, winking at Thomas.

It was a pleasant walk down to the pond after dinner. The sun was just above Mount Davidson, and there was enough of a breeze to cool things off.

"It would be fun to ride a bicycle down this hill," Alex said, "but not so great trying to ride it back up again."

"I'm not sure how many bicycles there are in 1869," said Bill, trying to remember.

"There's the pond!" Natalie said, pointing down the hill a little further, distracting him from his thoughts,

"Oh, right, that's the C & C pond." Bill said, his face brightening with the clear memory of having read about this particular swimming hole. "It was created by the California and the Consolidated-Virginia mines. They pump the water out of their mines, and then dump it into that pond. I remember reading about how it was a favorite swimming spot because the C & C mine dumped cold water into their pond. The other mines were dumping hot water from deeper shafts into their ponds."

"Is it safe?" Thomas asked. "Is it all right for them to go swimming in a pond the mines use?"

"I think it's OK," Bill answered. "The reason they have to pump water out of the mines is because they've dug so deep they're below the underground water table. Once that happens, the water above them seeps down into the mine shafts. It's the same water people get when they dig a well. It's not really great for drinking—it has a fair amount of alkaline in it—but I think it's OK to swim in for one summer."

"Should we be concerned about our drinking water?" Mary asked.

"That really depends on the season," Bill replied. "Right now, the town's water source is primarily melted snowpack from the Sierra Mountains that the Virginia and Gold Hill Water Company stores in big wooden tanks. Sometime this winter, though, the snowpack will stop melting, and the Virginia and Gold Hill Water Company will start adding water from the mines into the storage tanks. It won't taste the same, but it won't hurt you to drink it for a few months. In three or four years the town will build a new pipeline that will bring fresh water to Virginia City from Marlette Lake all year 'round."

"It sounds like the water is OK to swim in," Mary said, "but I'm still worried that there isn't a lifeguard or anything like that."

"Well, no," Bill replied, "That's true. There's no lifeguard."

"Nat's a really strong swimmer, and she's had pool safety training," Thomas reminded his wife. "I think it might be OK as long as she's there, don't you?"

"I think it would be a real challenge if she ever actually had to haul someone out of the pond," Mary said. "Remember the swimsuits girls have to wear? Basically, a dress with a pair of bloomers underneath. That's going to weigh a lot when it's wet. Plus, we'd be putting a lot of responsibility on Natalie's shoulders, don't you think?"

"I don't mind, Mom," Natalie said quickly. "I can wear one of Dad's t-shirts under the dress part of the bathing suit, so I could take the dress off if there was an emergency. People might be offended, but they'd get over it."

Mary thought about it for a minute. "Well, OK," she said, reluctantly, "but mostly because I don't want you guys sitting around the house all day, afraid to do anything. Please promise me, though, that you'll use your heads, and watch out for each other. There aren't many second chances in a place like this. You have to be careful."

"We will, Mom," Alex assured her.

"Yes, we will," Natalie and Benjamin agreed.

"OK, we'll be counting on that," Thomas said.

They stayed at the pond for a few more minutes, chatting, until Thomas said, "The sun is starting to

85

get pretty low. We should head back to the house before it sets."

"I'll race you!" Benjamin said to Alex and Natalie. They looked at each other for a second, and then bolted up the hill, running side by side, as fast as they could.

"Hey! That's not fair!" Benjamin called after them. He started running, trying to catch up, but didn't get very far before he was out of breath.

"It's really hard to run uphill!" he said.

In just a couple of minutes, Alex and Natalie slowed down to a walk and then stopped completely. Alex bent over and put his hands on his knees, taking deep breaths. After a minute of trying to look nonchalant, Natalie was doing the same thing.

When the adults caught up to them, Bill said, "The oxygen is thinner at this altitude. It's going to take a little longer for your bodies to get used to that. You should probably avoid uphill races for a few more days, until you're more adjusted to it."

"Good advice!" Alex said between breaths.

"Definitely!" Natalie agreed.

They finished the walk home at a slower pace, and then spent some time sitting on the front porch, enjoying the cool night air. The conversation was slow but filled with hope and satisfaction. They had accomplished a lot in just a few days, and they were proud of that.

After a couple of hours, everyone went to bed. Exhausted, they fell asleep quickly, barely noticing the continual noise of the mines.

Chapter 6

Getting Settled

"I think I know why they call it 'the crack of dawn,'" Thomas said early the next morning. "I'm pretty sure I heard all of my bones cracking when I got out of bed this morning." He sank gratefully into a chair at the kitchen table.

"Do we have coffee?" he asked Mary, who was standing on one of the chairs, measuring the window over the sink.

"We don't even have a coffeepot," Mary answered, looking at him over her shoulder, "but I'm going shopping for kitchen curtains today and I can look for one while I'm out. I'm sure I can figure out how to make coffee on the stove, but somebody will have to stoke the fire pretty early in the morning if you want it to be ready before you leave for the claim."

"I'm in favor of just getting our breakfast and our coffee at the Star Restaurant every morning," Bill said as he came into the kitchen.

"I think Caroline would be in favor of that, too," Mary said, stepping down from the chair with a smile.

"Oh, well," said Bill, blushing. "She's a very nice lady, and I enjoy talking to her."

"Mm-hmm." Mary said. "I saw a poster for a community dance next month. I'll bet if you asked her, she would go with you."

"I'm not much of a dancer," Bill said. "I'd probably stomp all over her feet."

"I could teach you a basic box step," Mary offered. "It's not fancy, but you can dance to just about any kind of music if you know the box step."

"Well, I'll think about it. I have some time. You said it's at the end of the month, right?"

"Yes, but I don't think you should wait too long to ask her if you're going to. I'm sure you're not the only guy in town who thinks Caroline is nice."

"I'll think about it," Bill repeated, as Natalie and Benjamin came straggling into the kitchen. "But now that everybody's awake, what do you say we head on over and get some breakfast?"

"Sounds good," Thomas said. "The walk over to the restaurant should help me stretch out these stiff joints."

"Mine, too," said Alex, placing his right foot up on a chair and bending down to stretch the muscles in the back of his leg. "Just give me a second," he said, switching legs so he could stretch out the left.

"It's hard to believe you guys are so much younger than I am," Bill joked, "but you'll be all right after a few more days of gold mining. It's the best exercise in the world. Keeps you limber and makes you rich at the same time!"

"That sounds good to me!" Thomas said. "Lead on. Breakfast first, and then we work on getting rich."

They all went out the front door, leaving Alex alone in the house.

"Sounds like a lot of shovel work to me," he said to the empty room, as he scooted his chair under the table. "Wait for me, guys!" he called, hurrying out the front door.

An hour later, Bill, Thomas, and Alex were headed out to their gold claim, while Mary, Natalie, and Benjamin went to the Territorial Enterprise building to buy a copy of the local newspaper. The front page was filled with advertisements, including one that caught Mary's attention.

"Oh, look!" she exclaimed, "Quong Hi Loy and Company, Chinese imports, vegetables, and herbs! It's down on Union Street. Let's go there first. Besides their vegetable selection, I want to check out their herbs and medicines. Some medicines we take for granted back in our time aren't available here, but the Chinese were known for having some very effective medicines long before the western world developed them."

"What kind of medicine are you talking about?" Natalie asked.

"Well, in particular, I'm thinking about antibiotics," Mary answered. "If I remember correctly, the Chinese developed an antibiotic from the mold that grows on soybeans. We don't need any right now, but it would be good to know if they have it, just in case."

Natalie and Benjamin followed their mother as she headed down the hill on Union Street.

"There sure are a lot of hills here," Benjamin said.

"Yes, there are," Mary agreed. "We're getting a workout!"

When they got to the Chinese market, Mary took a moment to remind her children not to touch anything and then opened the door. The aroma of spices and incense greeted them.

Natalie stepped inside first. "Mmm. It smells so good in here."

"I like the way it smells, too," said the lady who had come to see what they needed. She was Asian, and a little shorter than Mary. She wore a beautiful dark-blue silk dress that was embroidered with silver and gold thread. Her hair was black, and it was piled on top of her head in a bun. She walked so gracefully that she seemed almost to float. "I am Mrs. Yee. My family owns this store. May I help you?"

"Yes, thank you," said Mary, looking around at the neat rows of shelves and wicker baskets, all marked with Chinese characters. "I was wondering if you have medicine for an infection."

"Yes, of course," Mrs. Yee said, "We have that medicine. Would you like me to get it for you?"

"Oh, no, thank you," Mary said. "I don't need to buy it today, but I am glad to know I can buy it here if I need it. Today I would like to buy some vegetables. May I see them, please?"

"Oh, sure, sure. The vegetables are outside, still growing. Follow me," Mrs. Yee said, leading them through the back door of the shop to an enormous garden, where an elderly man was pulling weeds. When he saw he had visitors, he stood up and bowed slightly in their direction.

"That is my father-in-law," said Mrs. Yee. "He is an excellent farmer, but he doesn't speak much English. You point to what you want and he will tell me how much it costs."

With Mrs. Yee translating, Mary selected some yellow squash and a pound of green beans, which the man picked and placed in a small wooden box.

"Thank you so much," Mary said, as she paid for the produce. "I will be back to see you again, soon."

As they walked home, Natalie said, "They had so much interesting stuff in there, and it smelled so good!"

"And you sure can't buy vegetables that are any fresher than these," Mary said. "Right off the vine!"

When they got home, they unloaded their vegetables in the root cellar under the house, and then headed over to Ford's Dry Goods store for the rest of their shopping.

"Does every house in Virginia City have a root cellar?" Benjamin wanted to know, as they walked along C Street.

"I imagine they do," Mary answered. "There isn't any refrigeration here, except for the blocks of ice they cut from the lake up in the mountains during the winter. They store it in an icehouse, packed in sawdust, and then sell it in chunks. It gets pretty expensive to buy ice during the summer, so most people use a root cellar to store their vegetables and preserved meats. I remember reading about it when I was in high school. Some people put jams and jellies in the root cellar, too, along with the vegetables they've canned, so they can have them during the winter."

"So, it's basically an underground pantry," Natalie said.

"Right," Mary answered. "And that's why most houses would have one."

"I like it down there," Benjamin said. "It's nice and cool."

"Exactly," said Mary.

When they arrived at Ford's, Mary reminded herself that she was only there to buy curtains and a coffeepot. All sorts of other interesting items were on display, but she intended to stay focused on her mission. She went through the front door of the store without noticing the "Wanted" poster in the front window.

"Mom!" Natalie called to her mother, "You should come back and look at this."

Mary stepped back outside.

"It says the Stagecoach Bandit had an Irish accent and was wearing a green plaid handkerchief across his face," Natalie said, before Mary knew what she was talking about. "When I found the handkerchief at the parade, I talked to the man standing next to it, and he had an Irish accent."

Mary quickly scanned through the information on the poster, and said, "I know there are a lot of Irish people here, but I wonder how common it is to carry a green plaid handkerchief."

"I don't know," Natalie said, "I haven't seen any more handkerchiefs since that first day."

"We should to talk to your father and Uncle Bill about this tonight. It might be a good idea to let the Sheriff know where and when you found it."

Mary opened the door and went back inside. "Curtains and a coffeepot," she reminded herself. Then, looking down at the handkerchief wrapped around her shopping money, she added, "And maybe a small purse."

When they left the store twenty minutes later, Mary had purchased the curtains and coffeepot she came for, along with a drawstring bag called a 'reticule', which was, she had learned, the 1869 version of a purse. She had also purchased a book of fairy tales for Benjamin, and two small journal books with two pencils.

"You and Alex should start keeping journals about our time here," she said to Natalie. "This is quite an adventure, and some day you'll want to have something to remember it by."

"You mean to read after we get back home?" Natalie asked.

"Yes." Mary nodded. "To read after we get back home. But for right now, let's go hang these curtains in the home we have here."

Natalie knew her mother was doing her best to stay positive about their current situation, so she hurried her steps to catch up with her and slipped an arm around her waist.

"I guess you could call this a sideways walking hug," she said, with a smile.

"Just what I needed," Mary replied, smiling back at her.

Mary couldn't wait to show off the new kitchen curtains when the guys came home that evening. It surprised her when the door opened and Bill and Alex came in without Thomas. Then she saw the looks on their faces and knew something was wrong.

"What happened?" she asked, alarmed. "Where is Thomas?"

"The sheriff arrested him!" Alex said.

Natalie and Benjamin hurried into the living room to find out what was going on.

Mary was confused. She couldn't make sense of what her son was saying. "Arrested him?"

"We were heading home, walking up C Street," Bill said, "and then some guy starts saying 'There he is!' and he's waving a 'Wanted' poster. We had no idea what he was talking about, so we just kept walking."

"So we kept walking," Alex said, "and the guy is yelling, 'Somebody get the sheriff, I found the Stagecoach Bandit!' Then he starts yelling about reward money, and the next thing we know, the sheriff catches up to us, and asks Dad where he got the handkerchief he was wearing around his neck." Alex took a breath and continued, "So Dad explains that Natalie found it at the parade."

Mary looked at Bill. "And then what?"

"And then the sheriff asked Thomas where he was three weeks ago, when the stagecoach was robbed. We told him we were in San Francisco three weeks ago, and he asked if we could prove it, which, of course, we can't."

"So the sheriff said he was arresting Dad on suspicion of being the Stagecoach Bandit, and he took him to jail," Alex said, finishing the story.

"To jail?" Benjamin asked. His face crumpled, and he started to cry. Natalie wanted to cry, too, but she knew that getting Benjamin out of the room was the most helpful thing she could do at that moment. Her mother was going to need a little space.

Taking her brother by the hand, she lead him back to their bedroom, where she read stories to him until Uncle Bill knocked on the door and said it was time to go get some dinner.

Alex Taylor's Journal – July 11, 1869

Mom bought this journal for me so I won't forget this time in my life, but I'm pretty sure I don't need to write it down to remember it forever. Yesterday was the worst day ever! Dad got arrested! Just because he had the same kind of handkerchief as the Stagecoach Bandit, which wasn't even really his handkerchief. It was the one Natalie found at the Fourth of July parade. Dad tried to tell the sheriff, but then, when the sheriff asked Dad where he was when the stagecoach was robbed, Dad said he was in San Francisco, but he couldn't prove it. What was he supposed to say? It couldn't have been me because I was in a different century?

I don't know what to do. Mom is freaking out, and, to be honest, so am I. We have to wait for a judge to set bail for him. What if they hang him? Do they hang stagecoach robbers? I don't even know, and I'm afraid to ask.

Natalie Taylor's Journal – July 11, 1869

Dad got arrested because he had the green handkerchief around his neck, and it's all my fault. The sheriff said that nobody around here has ever seen a green handkerchief like that one, so it must belong to the bandit. Mom just sits at the table, not really talking or anything. Uncle Bill took us out to dinner, but Mom didn't want to go. Caroline was nice, and even gave everybody a free cookie, but I couldn't eat mine. I have to figure out a way to fix this.

Chapter 7

The Undertaker's Secret

Early the next morning, Bill, Mary, and Alex talked about what to do for Thomas. After a while, they agreed that working the claim was the best thing they could do. It could cost a lot of money to hire a defense lawyer, so they needed to keep looking for gold.

Natalie woke up shortly after Bill and Alex left for the claim. She did everything she could think of to make her mother feel better, but nothing seemed to help.

"Do you want a cup of tea?" she asked.

"Maybe later, but thank you for asking," Mary said.

"Did you sleep at all last night?"

"A little bit. I just don't know how we're going to prove your father's innocence. I blame myself for this. We should have gone straight over to the sheriff's office and told him about the handkerchief as soon as we saw that 'Wanted' poster."

"I've been thinking," Natalie said, "I should go back to the place where I found the handkerchief. I can look around and see if I can spot the man that was standing near it at the parade. I'm sure he's the one who dropped it, and he was not very nice when I asked if it was his. It was like he was angry that I thought it belonged to him, and that seems very suspicious now that I think about it. If it was his handkerchief, most likely, he's the real bandit!"

"Well, I guess that's a possibility," Mary replied, "but I'm worried about you going out on your own, looking for a man who might be the Stagecoach Bandit. You've already said he doesn't seem very nice."

"I'm just going to be walking down C Street in broad daylight, checking out the stores," Natalie said. "That seems pretty safe to me."

Mary looked at her daughter with concern. "You can go look around, but I want you to be very careful. Remember to use your head. OK? If you see the man, don't talk to him. Just come home and tell me where you saw him,"

"I will," Natalie replied.

She went out the front door, heading straight for the corner on C Street where she had found the handkerchief. Once she got there, she looked around. There was Beck's Hardware Store, Wells Fargo Bank, Ford's Dry Goods Store, and a store with a sign in the window that read, Francis McDonnell, Undertaker.

Undertaker? she said to herself. *What's that?*

Trying to figure out what an undertaker was, she stepped closer to the window and cupped her hands around her face so she could see inside.

"Coffins!" she exclaimed, taking a step back. "Creepy."

She stood outside the undertaker's window for several minutes, working up the courage to go inside. *Might as well get it over with*, she thought, and she quickly made up a cover story to explain her presence in the store. Once she was satisfied with her story she did her best to look sad, and then opened the door. A small bell on the door tinkled as she entered the room.

"I'll be there in just a minute," said a deep voice with an Irish accent, from another room.

Natalie had never seen a coffin up close before, and there were lots of them jammed into the small front room. Some were made of plain wood, and others were fancy, with silver or gold trim. The fanciest one of all was made of dark, gleaming wood, and it had gold latches and gold trim. Fascinated and scared, Natalie moved closer to study it. Curious about the inside, she lifted the lid just a little so she could peek inside. White satin lined the entire coffin, and there was a white satin pillow at one end. As she was quietly closing the lid, something shiny caught her eye. She lifted the lid back up and looked more carefully.

There was a small length of delicate gold chain sticking out from one edge of the pillow. Puzzled, she stared at it for a moment, but then quickly put the lid down when she heard footsteps approaching. She was turning to inspect a plain wooden coffin that was nearby when a man emerged from the back room. He was heavy set, and balding, and he looked at Natalie with practiced sympathy.

"How can I help you, young lady?" he asked. She heard the Irish brogue in his voice.

When she looked up at him, Natalie knew she wouldn't need to look any further for the man she had seen at the parade. He was standing right in front of her! Flustered, she started edging toward the door.

"M-m-my grandmother died. I'll ask my mom to come see you."

She felt the door handle behind her, so she turned and opened the door as quickly as she could. Once she was outside, she ran down C Street, turning onto the first side street she came to. When she was certain she was out of the man's sight, she made her way back to B Street and then ran the rest of the way home.

"Mom!" she shouted, as she burst through the front door.

"What in the world?" her mother asked, "I'm right here! The house is not that big."

"I found him!" Natalie exclaimed.

"What? The man at the parade? You did?"

"Yes, and he's an undertaker! His name is Francis McDonnell."

"An undertaker?" her mother asked, taken aback. After a pause she said, "I don't mean to sound discouraging, but it doesn't seem very likely that an undertaker is going to be out robbing stagecoaches in his spare time."

"I know," Natalie replied, "but he definitely doesn't seem like he's a very nice man, and maybe he doesn't get a lot of business. Maybe he robs stagecoaches when he needs more money. There is more than one undertaker in town, you know."

"True, but we can't prove the handkerchief was his, just because he was standing near it."

"I'm just so sure it's him. He was... creepy. I don't know how to explain it, but I really think he's the robber!"

"I know you're trying to help," Mary said, "but I doubt the sheriff would take you seriously. The man—Mr. McDonnell?—owns a respectable business in town. He's not a likely suspect, and the only thing you know for sure is that you saw him standing near a handkerchief. That's not enough to link him to the robberies."

Natalie's shoulders slumped, and she flopped down onto a kitchen chair.

"I guess you're right," she said, but her mind was racing.

"What's an undertaker? What are you guys talking about?" Benjamin asked, taking a seat at the kitchen table.

Before Mary could answer Benjamin's question, Natalie sat up straight and said, "I saw a gold chain that was partly hidden under a pillow inside one of the coffins. That could be evidence! Maybe that's where he hides the things he steals."

"You were opening the coffins?" Mary asked. "Why would you do that?"

"Well, uh, I don't know," Natalie confessed. "I was just curious."

"What's a coffin?" Benjamin asked.

Mary turned to Benjamin and said, "Later on, we'll have a conversation about undertakers and coffins, but right now need to go talk to the sheriff!"

That evening, Bill and Alex returned from their day of gold mining with exciting news.

"Check this out!" Alex exclaimed as soon as he walked through the front door. "I found it myself!"

He held his hand out so everyone could see the hefty gold nugget in his palm. Then he realized that his father was sitting at the kitchen table with an enormous smile on his face.

"That's a beauty!" Thomas said. "You found that at our claim?"

"Dad!" Alex exclaimed, rushing to give his father a hug. "You're home!"

Bill followed Alex in through the front door. "Thomas! You're here!"

He waited until Alex stepped out of the way, and then extended his hand, pulling Thomas into a hug and pounding him on the back several times.

"What happened?" he asked. "How did you get out of jail?"

"It turns out Natalie is quite the detective," Thomas said. "She figured out who the real bandit is, and she convinced the sheriff to check him out."

"I went back to the place where I found the handkerchief," Natalie explained, "to look for the man I saw at the parade. Then I looked inside one of the coffins at the undertaker's shop."

"You what?" exclaimed Alex, interrupting her story. "You went into an undertaker's shop and started opening up coffins?"

"Just the display coffins," Natalie assured him. "They were empty."

"Well, that's good," Alex said. "Because if they weren't empty, that would be weird. That would be worse than weird, actually."

"Well, yeah," Natalie acknowledged and then continued her story. "So I was checking out the stores near the corner where I found the handkerchief, and while I was in the undertaker's store I was looking in this fancy coffin, and I saw part of a gold chain sticking out from under the pillow."

"They have pillows in coffins?" Alex asked.

"Yes," Natalie said, throwing an exasperated look at her brother. "They have pillows in coffins."

"So, what happened after that?" Bill asked.

"OK," Natalie said, "so I saw part of a gold necklace tucked under the pillow, and I wondered why anybody would put jewelry under the pillow in a display coffin, unless they were using the coffin as a hiding place."

"So she came home and told me about it, and we went to the sheriff's office," Mary said, continuing the story. "Natalie told him what she had seen. The sheriff had us wait in his office while he went to check it out, and when he came back, he had the undertaker with him—in handcuffs!"

"The sheriff said that when he checked under the pillow, he saw a lot of jewelry," Natalie said, "so he lifted the edge of the satin liner and besides the jewelry, there were Wells Fargo money bags! It turned out that everything stolen during the last stagecoach robbery, including the payroll money for the mines, was hidden underneath the lining of that coffin!"

"So the undertaker is the Stagecoach Bandit," Bill said. "Who would have thought?"

"Precisely!" said Mary. "Thank goodness Natalie remembered him from the parade, or Thomas might still be sitting in jail."

"The sheriff released me about an hour ago and apologized," Thomas said. "All the charges against me have been dropped."

"That's awesome!" Alex said. He held up the nugget he had shown everyone earlier. "That means we won't need to use this beauty to post your bail!"

"That really is a beauty," Thomas said.

"Yep!" Alex said, nodding, with a big smile on his face. "I actually saw it right away when I dug it up. It was just sitting there in my shovel. At first I thought it was a piece of pyrite, but then I used my hand to shield it from the sun, the way Uncle Bill showed us, and it was still shiny, so I asked him to check it out, and, bam! I was right—it's gold!"

Alex stood there, smiling, while everyone in the family took turns holding the nugget.

"It's so heavy!" Natalie said, moving her hand up and down, testing its weight.

"That's another way you can tell it's real gold," Bill said. "Gold is very heavy."

"So are we rich now?" Benjamin asked.

Everyone laughed at Benjamin's question, enjoying the pure happiness of the moment. Thomas gave him a hug and said, "We aren't rich yet, but it's a good start!"

"Well, this has turned out to be a very good day!" Bill said. "I feel like celebrating! How about a nice steak dinner? After that, if the offer still stands, I would like to learn the box step. Will you teach it to me, Mary? I intend to ask Miss Caroline if she will accompany me to the community dance!"

"It will be my pleasure," Mary said with a smile. "I feel like dancing, too!"

Chapter 8

The Box Step

Over the next few weeks, the family fell into a routine. Bill, Thomas, and Alex went mining six days a week, taking Sundays off to rest. Mary spent her days teaching herself how to cook on a wood-burning stove and learning how to knit, while Natalie and Benjamin spent most of their afternoons at the C & C pond.

Alex got stronger and more tanned every day, and Natalie's hair grew out enough that people stopped asking about head lice. That made it much easier to make new friends while she and Benjamin were swimming. Every Sunday, Alex would join his brother and sister at the pond, and the three of them introduced the local children to games like Marco Polo and Water Tag.

One Sunday afternoon, Alex introduced everybody to the Cannonball, jumping into the water with both knees clutched to his chest. Then he proposed a weekly Cannonball Contest that quickly gained popularity at the pond. Whoever made the biggest splash won bragging rights for the rest of the week. Since this was potentially dangerous for the girls, who might have trouble swimming back up to the surface in their bulky swimwear, most of the girls served as judges. There was almost always a difference of opinion among the judges about the height of the splash, so they spent a great deal of time negotiating the score for each jump. This slowed the game down, and some of them could take all afternoon.

It wasn't long before Natalie and Benjamin were just as tanned as Alex, which caused Mary to worry about the lack of sunscreen. She experimented with various creams and lotions to see if any of them would block the sun's rays, and eventually, she hit on a combination of butter and zinc oxide that seemed to do the trick. All three of her children hated the greasy white potion.

"Come on, Mom," they would plead, "nobody else has white stuff all over their face. We look ridiculous!"

"You'll be glad we did this when you're old and your skin is healthy," she always responded, rubbing the mixture onto their exposed skin.

What Mary didn't know was that the butter in her homemade sunscreen made the whole gooey mixture melt away after fifteen minutes in the sun. By the time they walked from their house to the pond, most of it had already melted and dripped from their bodies. One quick wipe with a towel took care of the rest. Despite her best efforts, Mary's children had tans that deepened every day. Eventually she gave up on her homemade sunscreen, but she was still determined to protect her children's skin, so she became the 'hat police.'

Every time someone would leave the house Mary would call out, "Don't forget your hat!"

Knowing what was coming, Natalie and Alex made a game of it, and would mouth the words "Don't forget your hat" to each other when she reminded them.

"You mock me now," she would say, watching like a hawk while they put on their hats, "but you'll thank me later."

As the month of July passed by, Natalie and Benjamin spent most of their time swimming or playing games with the local children who came to the pond. After the arrest of the undertaker there weren't any more stagecoach robberies, which further convinced the sheriff he had arrested the right man. This, in turn, allowed Thomas to stop worrying about whether or not he was still under suspicion.

Caroline accepted Bill's invitation to the community dance, and in nervous anticipation of the event, he spent most of his evenings practicing the box step. Mary taught him the basic steps and he danced by himself in the living room, counting his steps, holding an imaginary dance partner in his arms.

"1, 2, 3, 4," he counted out loud, watching his feet as he made a box pattern.

"Do you want me to sing a song or something?" Natalie asked him one evening. "Maybe you should start practicing to some kind of music."

"I can't be thinking about music," Bill answered. "I'm counting! Do you want to dance with me?"

"Um, sure," she answered, watching his steps carefully. After a few minutes, she was able to make her steps match his.

"This is pretty easy!" she said.

"Easy for you," Bill said. "I have to lead, so you get the easy part."

"What do you mean?" Natalie asked. "It doesn't feel like you're leading. I'm just matching your steps."

"Trust me," Bill responded, "I'm leading."

"If you say so," Natalie replied, doubtfully.

During the last week of July, dancing practice was a nightly event. The whole Taylor family would join in, taking turns dancing with each other.

"We'll be the Divas of the Dance!" Natalie exclaimed. "We're getting pretty good at this!"

"As long as it's the box step!" Bill added, laughing.

On July 31st Bill was a nervous wreck. He had purchased a new shirt and a bow tie at the dry goods store for the occasion, but he couldn't figure out how to tie it.

"I don't get it," he complained. "I tie my shoes every day. Why is it so hard to tie a bow tie?"

"There's a trick to it," Mary said. "Let me help you."

"You're not the only one who has trouble with this," Thomas said to Bill from his seat at the kitchen table. "She'll be tying mine next. I've never been able to get the hang of it, either."

"Well, I really appreciate it," Bill said. "I was about to give up."

"We can't have that," Mary replied. "Not on your first date with Caroline!"

Bill blushed and didn't say anything more until Mary was finished with his tie.

"Thank you," he said, giving her a quick kiss on the cheek.

"You are very welcome." Turning to her husband, she said, "Next in line, please."

"Yes, ma'am," Thomas said, getting up from his chair. "That would be me."

By the time she finished everybody's bow ties, it was almost time to go to the dance. Bill was leaving a little earlier than the rest of the family, so he would have enough time to walk to Caroline's house and pick her up. After that, they would all meet up at Piper's Opera House.

"Good luck!" everyone said, as Bill headed towards the front door.

"You'll be fine," Mary assured him. "Just be yourself. She already likes that person."

Bill turned and smiled at her. "Thanks for the reminder."

Less than an hour later, they were all seated together at a large round table in the auditorium. Up on the stage, a band was playing a variety of lively musical tunes, and a few slower ones, too. For the first thirty minutes, they sat and watched other people dance.

"Well, that's enough sitting and watching!" Mary said, pushing back her chair. She stood up and offered her hand to her husband. "Would you like to dance with me?"

"As long as it's the box step," he said, taking her hand.

"Well of course! What else would it be?" she asked.

Thomas made a show of kissing the back of her hand. "Then let us make haste to the dance floor, my love."

Natalie looked over at Alex and pretended to stick her finger down her throat. "Oh, gag."

"Yeah, they're a bit much, sometimes," Alex agreed. He watched his parents dance for a minute, and then resumed his survey of the room.

"Do you know that girl?" he asked. "The one sitting at the table by the door?"

Natalie leaned to one side to get a better look. A pretty girl with light brown hair tied back in a blue ribbon was sitting at the table. Her dress was the same shade of blue as the ribbon, and each ruffle in her skirt had a border of white lace.

"I saw her once at the pond. I think her brother's name is Victor," she said, "and her name is... um," Natalie bowed her head for a moment and concentrated. "Sarah!" she exclaimed.

"Shh!" Alex turned his head slightly to see if there was any reaction at the girl's table. "You don't need to shout it."

"Sorry. I got excited when I remembered her name. Are you going to ask her to dance?"

"Maybe," he said. "I might."

"She's very pretty," Natalie said, "and that's a great dress. Her parents must have money."

"Yeah, maybe so," Alex said, not really listening to her.

"Well," Natalie said, "don't feel like you have to stay here and keep me company. Ben and I will be just fine together. Right, Ben?"

"I guess so," Benjamin answered, "but pretty soon I might ask Caroline to dance with me."

"Really?" Natalie asked.

"That's very sweet," Caroline said, "but I'd rather dance with the one that brought me." She

116

looked sideways at Bill and then quickly looked away.

"I only know the box step," Bill confessed to her.

"That's not a problem," Caroline replied. "The box step works for just about any kind of music."

"You know," Bill said, "I've heard that's true." He stood up and asked, "May I have this dance?"

"I thought you'd never ask," she answered, with a smile.

While the adults were dancing, Natalie turned her attention back to Sarah. Apparently, Sarah was just as interested in Alex because she kept glancing up to look at him. After a few minutes, Alex stood up from his chair and walked over to Sarah's table.

Natalie couldn't hear what he was saying, but she saw Sarah's father nodding, and then watched as Alex escorted her to the dance floor.

"Wow," she said to Benjamin. "Did you see that? He was, like, a perfect gentleman."

"Yep, I saw that," Benjamin replied.

When they reached the dance floor, Natalie watched her older brother do the box step with Sarah.

When did he become this guy? she wondered. *I barely recognize him.*

Alex was having similar thoughts as he was dancing with Sarah. At the same time, a small voice in his head was counting,

1, 2, 3, 4, 1, 2, 3, 4.

He could feel little pinpricks in his armpits as he started to perspire.

1, 2, 3, 4, 1, 2, 3, 4.

He concentrated on the steps. More than anything, he wanted to get it right and not embarrass himself. Her hand felt so delicate in his, and he could feel the laces of her corset under the fabric of her dress where his hand rested lightly on her back. He was getting a knot between his shoulder blades from standing so straight while he danced, but all of that faded away when his eyes met hers. She smiled at him, and he felt a thrill go through his body like an electrical charge. He had a few seconds to savor the feeling, and then the song was over. Taking his cue from the other people on the dance floor, he politely bowed his head to her, and then offered his arm to escort her back to her table.

Remembering all the times his mother had insisted on proper manners at the table, he pulled out Sarah's chair for her and waited for her to take her seat. Then he walked back to his family's table. His legs felt like jelly, and he quickly sat down.

"Oh, my gosh!" Natalie said. "That was totally perfect!"

"Yeah?" he asked, feeling a single bead of sweat slowly making its way down the center of his back.

"Yeah," Natalie said, in a rare moment of total solidarity with her brother. "You rocked it."

118

Alex smiled and said, "Thanks." The tension was starting to leave his body, and he relaxed back into his chair.

Natalie crossed her arms and sat back in her chair, too. She smiled at him. Then her eyes shifted to look over his shoulder.

"Uh, oh."

"What?"

"You have competition. Don't look! You'll see him in a minute without turning your head."

"What?" Alex asked again, trying to understand what his sister was telling him.

"Some other guy just asked Sarah to dance. They're walking over to the dance floor now."

Following his sister's instructions, Alex sat perfectly still until Sarah and her new dance partner came into view. Doing his best to look casual about it, he watched them dance for a few seconds, and then looked away.

"She looks bored," Natalie said.

Looking back at his sister, he asked, "Do you think so?"

"Yeah, I think so," she said. "I think she's way more interested in you than she is in that guy."

Alex nodded slightly and said, "Cool."

When the band started playing the next song, Sarah went back to her seat. Natalie turned to her little brother and said, "What do you think, dude? Do you want to see if we can do the box step?"

"Sure," Benjamin said. He stood up from his chair and walked around the table to offer his arm.

"Mom is probably so proud of you right now," Natalie said, reaching down to lay her hand on top of his arm as they walked to the dance floor.

Natalie Taylor's Journal – July 31, 1869

It's after midnight and I should be asleep, but I want to write about the community dance tonight. Alex danced with a girl named Sarah, and I think they really like each other. He danced with her twice. Once at the beginning of the dance and once at the end. Uncle Bill danced with Caroline lots of times, and they both looked so happy. I really like her, and she makes Uncle Bill smile. Mom and Dad seemed pretty happy tonight, too. I think it was the best time we've had since we've been here.

P.S. Mom was right – the box step works for almost any kind of music!

Alex Taylor's Journal – August 1, 1869

We went to the community dance last night, and it was pretty cool. I met a girl named Sarah, and we danced a couple times. She has light brown hair and brown eyes. She's going to be in eighth grade this year, so she will probably be in my class.

Dad and Uncle Bill said that I can take Saturdays AND Sundays off for the rest of the summer. We've been getting a lot of gold at our claims, which is awesome. It helps a lot that Uncle Bill knows where we should dig, but even if you know where to dig, it's still hard work. I'm glad I get to take the whole weekend off from now on. I guess we have enough gold that everybody has stopped worrying about money.

I'm pretty sure we're going to the C & C pond today to go swimming. I remember that Natalie said Sarah and her brother went there once.

Chapter 9

Summer Days

August was the hottest month of the year in Virginia City, but it was also exciting, because so many entertainment acts came to town. Brightly colored posters seemed to be everywhere, stuck to lampposts and shop windows, and the advertising section of the local newspaper took up more space every day.

"Mom, can we go see some of the shows at Piper's Opera House?" Natalie asked. "Everybody at the pond talks about the shows they've seen. The tickets are fifty cents each."

"What kinds of shows do they have?" Mary asked.

Natalie picked up the newspaper. "Here are a couple of advertisements for shows this month," she said, smoothing the paper out on the kitchen table for her mother to see.

"Can we go see the contortionist?" she asked. "That one looks cool. Maybe a little creepy, but still kind of cool."

"I'd be OK with seeing that one. It's Miss Forrestell's act. I've seen her posters in town. They call her the 'India Rubber Woman' because of the way she twists her body around. Her act will be different than the shows we're used to seeing, but, then, a lot of things are different here."

"So we can go?"

"Sure. We can go. We'll see if your father and brothers want to come, too."

"Thanks, Mom!" Natalie said. She headed back to the bedroom she shared with her brothers to put on her "swimming dress." She and Benjamin had been going to the pond every day, and she was really enjoying it. Benjamin's friend Yancy was also there every day, and the other swimming pond 'regulars' were starting to look familiar. Every time she saw Yancy, she wondered what happened to his little toe, but Benjamin never remembered to ask him about it. If he didn't ask pretty soon, she decided she would do it herself.

It only took a few minutes to get ready, and then she and Benjamin were on their way to the pond. As usual, Benjamin was chattering away, and Natalie was only sort of listening to him.

".... Teddy is eleven years old," he said. "He has two sisters and one brother, but only his brother comes to the pond. His brother's name is Elliott, and he's eight years old. I like Elliott. Sometimes we catch grasshoppers. I would like to get a string so I could have a pet grasshopper. I would name him 'Jumper.'"

"Does your brain ever take a rest?" Natalie asked, as the pond came into view.

"Nope!" Benjamin said, proudly. "It just goes on and on, all the time."

"Yeah, I noticed that," Natalie said, breaking into a run.

"Hey! Wait up!" Benjamin called, running after her.

"I need a break from hearing about every single thing that goes on in your brain!" she shouted back to him.

"I don't know how to take a break from my brain." Benjamin shouted back, slowing to a walk. "I don't think you can do that."

Natalie ran the rest of the way to the pond, and then jumped into the water, making sure she cleared the muddy ledge concealed under the grass at the edge of the pond. The first time they had come swimming, it shocked her when her second step into the pond had sent her plunging into ten feet of water. Luckily, Benjamin hadn't stepped in yet, and she'd had a chance to warn him. For the next couple of days after that they had both been cautious about getting in and out of the pond, but now they were familiar with its narrow ledges.

"Come on in!" she called out to Benjamin when he was close enough to hear her.

"I'm coming!" he said, as he took off his shoes. "Cannonball!" he shouted, running towards the pond.

Natalie quickly turned away and closed her eyes tight, so the splash of water wouldn't hit her in the face. A second later, Benjamin's head popped up next to her. He stayed there for a minute, treading water and shaking his wet hair out of his eyes.

"I saw Yancy and Elliot on the other side of the pond," he told her.

"Oh, good. Then you'll have someone to play with."

"Yep. I'm going to go over there and see what they're doing."

"OK," Natalie said. "Have fun!"

For the next twenty minutes, Natalie swam laps in the pond. She missed her swim goggles and spandex bathing suit, but reminded herself that swimming laps in a full dress had to be making her stronger.

When we get back, she thought, *I'm going to blow my whole swim team out of the water. LOL. Blow them out of the water.*

She kept that thought in her head when she started getting tired and pushed herself to do two more laps. Finally, she'd had enough, and she headed for a grassy spot at the narrow end of the pond.

Out of the water, her "swimming dress" felt like it weighed a ton. Water cascaded down her skirt and splashed around her feet. She stood and watched for a few seconds, wondering why her mother worried about sunscreen when so much of her skin was covered by her bathing suit.

Sighing, she wrung out the skirt as best she could, and then found a place to sit on the grass, near a boy who was reading a book. He was wearing a short jacket with knickers and white socks. She had seen him at the pond several times before, but they had never spoken.

"You don't look like you're dressed to go swimming," she said to him.

"No, I'm not going to swim today. I have asthma. It gets to me, sometimes," he explained, "and I can't go swimming."

"Oh, I'm sorry," Natalie said. "Why do you come to the pond if you can't swim?"

"It's OK. I like to swim, but I like to sit here and read, too. Besides, my brother, Elliott, wanted to swim today, and he's too young to come by himself. I don't mind."

"Your brother's name is Elliott?" Natalie asked. "I think he and Yancy are playing with my brother, Ben."

"Oh, yes," said the boy. "I've heard him talking about Ben and Yancy. Ben is new here, I think."

"Yes, he is," Natalie said. "I'm his sister." She held out her hand and said, "Pleased to meet you. My name is Natalie."

The boy shook her hand and said, "My name is Teddy."

"Teddy? Like, a teddy bear?" Natalie asked.

"What?" Teddy asked. "I don't think I know what a teddy... bear is."

Natalie felt the blood rush to her face. She wasn't sure when teddy bears had been invented.

"Oh, never mind," she said. "I think of funny things sometimes. It's nice to meet you, Teddy."

"Likewise," said Teddy. "Where did you and Ben come from?"

"We came from San Francisco," she said, remembering the cover story her parents had agreed they would all tell. "I have an older brother, too. His name is Alex."

"From San Francisco?" Teddy asked. "I've been to San Francisco many times! Have you ever been to the Cliff House?"

"Um, no, I haven't," Natalie replied.

"The California Theatre?"

"No."

"Have you seen the Grand Hotel?"

"Nope. I haven't been there, either." Trying to distract him, she asked, "Have you been to Piper's Opera House?"

"Yes!" Teddy exclaimed. "I saw Othello there, just the other day. What did you see?"

"Oh," Natalie said, "I went to the community dance there, but I haven't actually seen a performance, yet."

Teddy looked puzzled. "How long have you been here?" he asked. "You haven't seen very much."

"I've been to Quong Hi Loy and Company, Chinese Imports, over on Union Street," Natalie said, which made them both burst out laughing.

Teddy gasped for air. "Stop," he pleaded. "I really do have asthma. I need to catch my breath."

"Oh, I'm sorry," Natalie said. "I'll just sit here quietly."

Still smiling, they sat together on the grass and waited for their giggles to go away.

"I need to check on my brother pretty soon," Natalie said after a few minutes.

"Actually, I need to check on my brother, too." They both stood up and brushed off their clothes.

"What do you know about Yancy's little toe?" Natalie asked, hoping she would finally get an answer.

Teddy looked at her curiously. "I don't know anything about Yancy's little toe. Why do you ask?"

"Because it's missing," Natalie said.

"What?" Teddy said, and then he laughed again. "Sakes alive, please, no." He put his hand on her shoulder and bent at the waist, laughing, coughing, and trying to catch his breath at the same time.

Natalie stood still while Teddy leaned against her. She was afraid to say anything else about Yancy and his missing toe.

"Maybe we can talk about it another time," she said, as she patted him on the back.

"Yes, another time," Teddy agreed. "Let's do that."

At dinner that night, Natalie told her parents about Teddy. "I met him at the C & C pond. He's a little younger than I am, but I like him."

"That's nice," Mary said. "I've been hoping you would make friends while we're here. Maybe we can invite him over for lunch one day."

"Yeah, maybe," Natalie said. "I don't really know him well enough to invite him over for lunch yet, but maybe later. Thanks for the offer, though."

"Well, speaking of new friends," Mary said, turning to Bill, "are you and Caroline planning to go out again?"

"Yes, we are," Bill answered. "I asked her to go on a picnic with me down Six Mile Canyon."

"That's great!" Mary exclaimed. "When are you going?"

"This Saturday. I'm going to pick up some ready-made sandwiches at the market, and maybe get some pickles."

"That sounds like a very nice first date," Mary said.

"Second date," Bill corrected her.

"Second date. Right," Mary said. "What are you planning to wear?"

Bill looked down at the clothes he was wearing, and said, "I'm just going to wear my regular clothes."

"You'll need a blanket to sit on," Mary said. "Do you have a blanket?"

Running his hand across the top of his head, Bill said, "I'm just going to take the blanket from my bed."

"Maybe we should let Bill plan his own date," said Thomas, jumping into the conversation. "It sounds like he has everything under control."

"I'm just trying to help," Mary said. She reached across the table and put her hand on Bill's arm. "If there's anything I can do—anything at all—just let me know."

Bill looked up at her. "You remember I was married for thirty years, right? I think I'll be OK."

"Of course you will," Mary said, settling back in her chair and adjusting the napkin in her lap. "Next Saturday, then! I'm excited for you!"

"Thank you," Bill said.

"So it's a picnic lunch. What time are you picking her up?"

"Mary!" Thomas exclaimed. "Just let him be!"

"Oh, all right," she said, looking a little annoyed, "but you sure are spoiling this for me."

Thomas turned to Bill and said, "I'm gonna start clearing the table now. You're on your own, buddy."

"Go ahead. Leave me here. Save yourself." Bill said, jokingly. Both men laughed, and Mary crossed her arms.

"I don't know why I bother, sometimes," she said, shaking her head.

Alex Taylor's Journal – August 13, 1869

So far I haven't seen Sarah at the C & C pond. Maybe her family went out of town. Or maybe it's too hot for her now.

We went to see the India Rubber Woman at Piper's Opera House on Monday, and it was weird. I thought she would be doing gymnastics stuff, like the rings or the uneven parallel bars, but it was more like she turned herself into a pretzel. Then she did this thing with a really heavy anvil on her stomach, which was kind of freaky. I don't know how she came up with the idea of doing that stuff and turning it into a show.

<u>*Natalie Taylor's Journal – August 13, 1869*</u>

Uncle Bill and Caroline are going to watch the Fireman's Tournament together tomorrow, and then they are going out for dinner at a fancy restaurant. I think she's really nice, and I'm glad Uncle Bill is happy, but I wonder if he's thought about how sad he'll be in December – assuming that they are still seeing each other by then. I worry that he's going to get his heart broken, but I guess there isn't much I can do about that.

But, like I was saying, the Fireman's Tournament is tomorrow. There are TWELVE fire stations in this town! That's a lot of fire stations, but there are a lot of fires here, and it usually takes two or three stations to put a fire out. Anyway, they are going to have a water shooting competition and a foot race against each other to see who can run the fastest from the Young America Engine House on C Street to the Knickerbocker Engine House on D Street. They have to carry 500 feet of firehose while they're running. The station that wins will get a silver trumpet, which seems like a weird prize to me. Just about everybody in town is betting on this. Even Teddy asked me if I wanted to bet a nickel, which I didn't, because I don't want to take a chance on losing.

We went to see the India Rubber Woman act at Piper's Opera House a few days ago. It was very strange, but Piper's Opera House is really nice. Now I can tell Teddy I've seen a performance there. Maybe we can go to a different kind of performance sometime soon. Like, maybe somebody who can sing. Or a band, or something like that.

Chapter 10

The Circus Comes To Town

"Hurry, hurry, hurry! Step right up!" called the man standing at the entrance to the big top tent. He was wearing a red jacket with big brass buttons and black pants. A black stovepipe hat completed his outfit, and the color was an exact match for his handlebar mustache, curled to perfection on either side of his mouth.

"Right this way, ladies and gentlemen," he shouted, beckoning people to come closer.

"Come see Miss Gracie, the World-Famous Trapeze Artist! Watch the Strongman bend iron bars and lift over two hundred pounds with one arm! You will marvel at the death-defying leaps and somersaults of our lovely female Equestrian Team! Come see our Zebras and Lions and Tigers! Come see the Elephants! Hurry, hurry, hurry! Step right up!"

"Do you see that tent over there, to the right of the big top tent?" Alex asked Natalie and Benjamin as they followed Uncle Bill, Caroline, and their parents down the hill to E Street. "That's where they're keeping the animals. I watched them unload the tigers and zebras, and I'm pretty sure I heard an elephant."

"Teddy said that he heard they have *sixty* horses!" Natalie said. "That's a lot of horses!"

"Wow! Sixty horses!" Benjamin exclaimed. "I'd like to see sixty horses."

"I don't think they could fit sixty horses into that tent," Alex said. "Maybe they keep them somewhere else."

"I'm looking forward to the trapeze acts," Natalie said.

"Me, too," said Benjamin. "All of my friends are going to be there."

"All of your friends?" Alex asked. "Which friends?"

"My friends from swimming," Benjamin replied. "Yancy and Elliot."

"Oh, all two of your friends," Alex said.

Natalie shot her older brother a look. "Don't be mean. You don't need to prove that you're ..." she fumbled for the right word, "*older*."

"I wasn't being mean," Alex said, walking faster, trying to put an end to the conversation. Natalie lifted her skirt up a few inches so she could keep up with him.

"Yes, you were. And for no reason at all, as far as I can tell. If anybody has a right to be cranky, it should be me. You pretty much get to wear regular clothes every day and do regular stuff. You don't have to wear a long skirt, or wear your hair a certain way, and you mostly get treated like an adult. It's not fair."

Alex kept walking, hoping she was finished.

"I'm over here, practically dying of heatstroke," she continued, "because I have to wear these stupid long skirts. Even when I'm swimming, I have to wear a freaking dress, Alex!" She dropped her skirt and slowed her steps. "It's so much easier for boys here."

Alex slowed down, too. "OK. OK. I'm sorry," he said, sounding almost sincere.

They were getting close to the entrance of the big top tent where the adults were waiting, and he was eager to put an end to the flare-up. "You're right. I'm sorry. I didn't mean to start an argument." He paused, and then said, "Truce? I'll share my popcorn with you guys, OK?"

Natalie kept frowning at him for a few more seconds and then relented. "OK. I guess I'm just hot. We can have a truce, but I want extra butter on the popcorn, if they have it. Ben does, too." She turned to see if Benjamin agreed and then realized that he wasn't there.

"Alex, do you see Ben?" she asked.

"What?" Alex asked, exasperated. "He was just here."

"Ben!" Natalie called, as she scanned the crowd behind them.

"What the heck?" Alex said, as he and Natalie turned and headed back in the direction they had come from.

"Alex, Natalie, what's going on?" Thomas called out to them from the entrance to the big top.

"We can't find Ben," Alex called back to him.

All four of the adults left the entrance to the tent and joined Alex and Natalie.

"He was just here a second ago," Natalie said. "He can't be very far away."

Raising his voice, Thomas called his youngest son's name. They all waited, but there was no response.

"When was the last time you saw him?" Mary asked.

Natalie thought for a second. "We were about halfway between D and E Streets," she said. "We were talking about the circus animals."

Thomas took charge. "OK, everybody, we need to fan out and look for him. We'll meet back at this spot in ten minutes. If you find him sooner, though, come back here right away."

"Natalie, go back to the house and check to see if he went home. Alex, go check around the animal tent. Caroline, can you look near the food vendors, and Mary, will you check the privies?"

"The circus is sponsoring another Firemen's Race during today's performance," Bill said, "I'll go ask the firemen that are here to help us look."

"Thank you." Thomas said. "That's a good idea."

As soon as they had their assignments, everyone left to check his or her designated area.

Thomas stood there for a moment, alone, trying to imagine where Benjamin might go. What would make him wander off without saying anything?

"Ben!" he called out one more time, hoping his son might hear him. When there was no response, he started walking to the spot where Natalie and Alex said they had last seen him—between D and E Streets.

"Ben!" he called again, scanning the area as he walked. Behind him, Bill and several firemen came out of the big top tent.

When Thomas reached E Street, he stopped and looked around. There were several houses lining the street, and he wondered if Yancy or Elliott lived nearby. Would Benjamin go to a friend's house and not tell somebody? On the way to the circus? It seemed very unlikely to Thomas. He started walking up the hill towards D Street, searching for his son as he walked. Then a slight movement to his right caught his attention. He stopped and looked around.

A dog barked, and he stepped closer to the sound. The dog barked again, and Thomas heard Benjamin's voice, telling the dog to be quiet. Looking to his right, he saw an unhitched wagon parked next to a house. Taking a few steps toward it, he bent down and peered into the shadowy area below it.

140

Under the wagon, Benjamin was sitting cross-legged in the dirt, clutching a small dog with matted fur.

"He kept following me, and I wanted to tie him up so he would wait for me, but I couldn't find anything to tie him with," Benjamin said, looking up at his father with a fearful expression on his face. "I thought it would only take a minute, and I was going to catch up to Nat and Alex."

Relieved, Thomas sat down on the ground next to the wagon, facing his son.

"Everybody's looking for you," he said. "That dog is a stray. You should let him go."

"He's not a stray," Benjamin protested. "He hangs around our house all the time. Sometimes I give him part of my food."

"Well, that explains why he hangs around our house all the time," Thomas said, reaching under the wagon to offer Benjamin a hand. "Just let him go. He'll be fine. We need to let everybody know you're OK."

Benjamin took his father's hand and scooted out from under the wagon. "His name is Pete," he said as he stood up.

"You named him?" Thomas asked, staring down at the scruffy animal.

"Yes," Benjamin answered hesitantly. He wasn't sure how much trouble he was in, or if it might be worse, because he had named the dog.

"Well, I'm sure Pete can take care of himself," Thomas said. "It looks like he's been doing that for quite a while. Let's go."

"Stay, Pete, stay!" Benjamin said, forcefully, to the dog.

"Come on," Thomas said. "We need to tell everyone they can stop looking for you."

Benjamin hurried to keep up with his father, but he was having no luck getting Pete to 'stay.' The little dog followed right behind them, wagging his tail.

"Just ignore him," Thomas said. Seeing several people at the designated meeting spot, he called out, "I found him!"

Mary broke away from the group and hurried to intercept them. "Oh, thank goodness! You had me worried to death, young man!" she said.

Right behind her, Natalie said, "Me, too! I kept thinking an elephant might have stepped on you."

"I'm sorry," Benjamin said, "I was trying to figure out what to do about Pete."

"Pete?" Alex asked, as the rest of the group gathered around.

"Apparently, Benjamin has been feeding a stray dog, and now it follows him around," Thomas responded, looking at Mary.

Mary sighed. "I should have seen that coming," she said. "Ever since I tossed that burned batch of bacon into the street, we've had two or three dogs

142

hanging around the house. I've been hoping they'd give up and move on."

"They did all go away, except for Pete," Benjamin said.

"Because you fed him," Thomas said disapprovingly.

"Well, I'm sure Pete is a very resourceful dog," Mary said. "He'll be fine on his own while we go see the circus. Come on, we still have enough time to see the opening act."

Thomas and Bill stayed behind for a few minutes to shake hands with the firemen who had volunteered to help look for Benjamin. Then they joined Caroline and the rest of the family inside the tent. Pete sat outside the tent for a few minutes and then wandered away.

Inside the tent, there were two circus rings, and the action started when two women, who were juggling knives, each rode two horses into one of the rings. Their horses ran around each ring several times while the women continued their death-defying juggling acts. When they finished, several trapeze artists in blue tights ran out and started climbing up the tall poles to the platforms high above the crowd.

As the trapeze artists began their aerial performances overhead, two men each led four tigers into each of the two rings. They cracked their whips in unison, and the tigers all stood on their hind legs, turning themselves around in a circle.

For the next hour and a half, one act followed another. Clowns followed the tigers and the trapeze act, a cowboy cattle drive followed the clowns, and trained elephants followed the cowboys. When it came time for the Fireman's Race, the Taylors cheered as loudly as they could, and when the race was over, they stood up and applauded the winner. He had completed five laps around one of the circus rings in just thirty-five seconds, beating his closest competitor by one second.

When the circus was over, everyone agreed it was worth every penny they had paid for the tickets.

"I can't wait for the next circus!" Benjamin exclaimed as they were walking home. "That was so fun!"

When they approached the house, Thomas was the first to notice the visitor that was waiting for them on the front porch, wagging his tail.

"Pete!" Benjamin exclaimed. "I'm glad you're OK."

Mary and Thomas exchanged looks.

"You need to leave him outside," Mary said, "but if he's still here in the morning, we'll give him a bath and see who he is underneath all that dirt and matted fur."

Benjamin's face lit up. "Did you hear that, Pete? You can sleep here on the porch tonight, OK, boy?"

Pete continued to sit, wagging his tail. For the rest of the evening, Benjamin checked on the little stray, reminding him he should stay on the porch until morning. This time, Pete seemed to understand. When the sun rose the next morning, Benjamin was delighted to find that the dog was still there, curled up in a ball, sleeping by the front door.

After breakfast, Benjamin and his mother gave Pete a bath in a metal washtub on the front porch. By the time they finished, there was a layer of mud at the bottom of the tub, and Pete was a lighter shade of brown than he was when they started. Brushing out his matted fur was more of a challenge, but eventually, they managed to get him completely de-tangled.

"Look at you!" Benjamin's mother exclaimed when they had finished. "You're a handsome boy, aren't you?"

Pete wagged his tail and barked once, as if to say he agreed with her. After that, Pete was an official member of the Taylor family—at least temporarily. They taught him some manners, and every now and then they talked about finding a local family to adopt him before they went home on December 26th.

Chapter 11

Future Famous Authors

For the rest of August, Caroline and Bill saw each other almost every evening, and Caroline began stopping by the Taylor house regularly when she finished her shift at the restaurant. It was clear to Caroline that Mary was still learning how to cook on the wood-burning stove, so she always stayed at the house long enough to lend a hand with dinner preparations. She wondered why Mary was just now learning to cook, but she didn't want to pry. Instead, she did her best to be helpful. Today she was there to help her friend bake a loaf of bread.

"I started the fire a couple of hours ago," Mary said, when Caroline came to the door. "It's just a small fire, like you said."

Caroline went to the oven and opened the bottom door so she could see the fire. "That's perfect," she said. "The oven should be heating up evenly. Do you have the flour ready?"

Mary nodded, and Caroline opened the oven door above the fire door. Mary tossed in a handful of flour, and they both watched to see what would happen. If the flour stayed white, or turned just slightly yellow, they would know the oven wasn't ready. If it quickly turned dark, or if it burned right away, they would know the oven was too hot, and they should wait for the fire to die down a bit.

They watched the flour intently, not saying a word. After a minute, it began to change from white to golden brown, and then slowly darkened.

"Bully!" exclaimed Caroline. "Are you soaking a piece of wood?"

"Yes," Mary said, nodding and smiling at Caroline's enthusiasm. 'Bully' was one of Caroline's favorite words. Mary had figured out some time ago that it meant, 'great!', but it still struck her as funny every time she heard Caroline say it.

"I've had a piece of wood soaking over here, in the bucket, ever since I started the fire," Mary said.

"All right, then." Caroline took an apron down from a hook on the kitchen wall and tied it around herself. "Let's get started."

Mary reached across the counter for a bowl covered with a towel and pulled it closer. She sprinkled a little flour on the counter, and then pulled the towel away from the bowl, scooping out a ball of dough. Caroline watched approvingly as Mary placed the dough on the floured surface and pushed down on it. For the next few minutes, she pushed and folded the dough, kneading it until it felt stretchy and smooth. When she was finished, she put the dough in a pan and carried it to the oven.

"Don't forget the piece of wood you've been soaking," Caroline reminded her.

"Right! Thank you for reminding me."

Caroline had explained that putting a piece of wet wood at the back of the oven kept things from drying out too much while they were cooking. After placing the piece of wet wood at the back, Mary put the pan full of dough in the center of the oven and closed the door.

She glanced at the clock on the wall and said, "Twenty minutes, right?"

"Right," Caroline answered. "You should check it in twenty minutes to see if it's ready. You can always give it a few more minutes if it needs it."

"I can't thank you enough for helping me," Mary said. "Can you stay for a little while? I made some lemonade. Would you like a glass?"

"That sounds wonderful," Caroline said, pulling out a chair from the kitchen table and taking a seat.

The two women sat and chatted as the house filled with the aroma of freshly baked bread. When Mary took the loaf from the oven, Caroline declared that it was "a daisy," which Mary assumed was a good thing. Not for the first time, she wished she had a dictionary of 1869 slang, so she could be sure of what people were saying to her.

Mary cut two slices from the warm loaf and gave one slice to Caroline.

"Delicious!" Caroline declared, and Mary had to agree.

"You are always so helpful," Mary said. "If I can ever return the favor, please let me know."

"Don't even worry about it," Caroline said. "That's what friends are for."

It turned out that Mary would be able to return the favor less than a week later. Early in the morning, there was a knock at the door, and she opened it up to find a small boy standing on the porch.

"Are you Miss Mary?" he asked.

"Yes, I am," Mary responded, puzzled by the inquiry.

"Miss Caroline at the Star Restaurant sent me to ask if you have time this morning to help her with the morning rush," the boy said, carefully, as though he had memorized the message.

"Caroline needs my help at the restaurant?" Mary asked.

"Yes, ma'am," the boy nodded.

"Please tell her I'll be right there," Mary said. She watched as the boy turned and ran down the street towards the restaurant.

"Natalie!" she called, sitting down to put her shoes on. "I'm going to go help Caroline at the restaurant for a little while."

"OK," Natalie called back from the bedroom she shared with her brothers. "I'm going to take Ben to the pond, OK?"

As Mary headed out the front door, she answered, "That's fine. Be safe!"

Two blocks away from the restaurant, she could see why Caroline had asked for help. There were at least twenty people waiting in line outside the restaurant.

"Oh my goodness," she said, and quickened her pace. "Looks like it's a very busy morning!"

Caroline looked up when Mary came through the restaurant door and gave her a grateful smile. As soon as she finished with the customers she was serving, she met Mary in the kitchen.

"This is the busiest I've ever seen it!" Caroline said.

"I saw the line outside," Mary said. "There are another twenty people out there."

"Thank you for coming. We have an extra cook to help, but I can't keep up with the tables by myself, and I haven't been able to find anyone else to help. I hope you're wearing comfortable shoes! Just get an apron and start taking orders. I'll be right here if you have questions."

Mary nodded and reached for an apron.

"Thank you, Sweet Pea!" Caroline said, picking up the next order of food.

It took a little while for Mary to get into the rhythm of taking orders and serving food, but she got better at it as the morning progressed. By the time the restaurant was shifting from breakfast to lunch, she had become a competent waitress, but she was ready to take a break.

"Just one more table," she thought, as two distinguished-looking gentlemen came in. She watched them walk to an empty table, thinking that one of them looked familiar, but she couldn't remember where she might have seen him before. She was still trying to figure it out when she brought silverware and napkins to their table.

"Are you here for breakfast, or will you be wanting lunch?" she asked.

"Breakfast, I think," the man replied. Looking at his companion, he asked, "What do you say, William? The breakfast special?"

"Sounds good, Sam," the man nodded. "Although I'm a lot hungrier for news than I am for breakfast. I want to know everything about your fiancée, your wedding plans, and your escapades since you left the *Territorial Enterprise*."

Suddenly, Mary knew why the first man looked so familiar. He was Samuel Clemens, the famous writer! Using the pen name 'Mark Twain,' he was going to write several famous books, including *Roughing It* and *Tom Sawyer*. Mary stood there, staring at the man in amazement. She couldn't believe Mark Twain was sitting right in front of her.

"Are you all right, Miss?" he asked.

Flustered, Mary said, "Mary. Mary Taylor. Pleased to meet you. Oh, yes, Mr. Clemens, I'm just fine, thank you! I'll go and get your food now. It'll just be a minute. Thank you," she said, as she backed away from the table. "Thank you."

She turned and hurried into the kitchen, and then stood there for a minute, biting down on her knuckle to keep herself from bursting with excitement. She was serving breakfast to Mark Twain! Looking back at the table, she realized the man seated with him must be his good friend, William Wright, the reporter for the *Territorial Enterprise* newspaper who used the pen name "Dan DeQuille." Mr. Wright would also be a well-known author one day. Mary willed herself to be calm.

They're just regular people, she said to herself as she carried their breakfasts across the dining room. She tried not to interrupt their conversation, and set each man's plate in front of him, carefully. Once her mission was complete, she took a step back and stood there, smiling.

After a few seconds, they stopped chatting and looked up at her. "Are you all right?" Mr. Clemens asked.

"Oh! Oh, yes!" she said, taking a step back from the table. She could feel her face turning red.

"I think we have everything we need," he said, looking at her with a quizzical expression on his face.

"Of course. If you need anything, just let me know," she said, taking another step backwards, "Even though I know you just said you don't need anything right now," she babbled. Waving her arm vaguely behind her, she continued, "I'll just be over there."

She nodded to them, and finally retreated to the kitchen, where she grabbed onto the countertop to steady herself.

"You're acting like a perfect idiot!" she said to herself in a whisper. "Stop it!"

Caroline came into the kitchen just in time to hear Mary whispering something. "Are you all right?" Caroline asked. "You looked flushed."

Mary burst out laughing, and said, "Oh, yes, I'm just fine."

Caroline squinted and looked at Mary more closely. "Are you sure? You really do look flushed."

"I'm fine," Mary assured her, taking a deep breath. "Just fine! Did you know that Samuel Clemens and William Wright are here?"

Caroline looked toward the dining room and said, "Oh, yes, it's nice to see Mr. Clemens again. Those two were chuckaboos when Mr. Clemens was working at the *Territorial Enterprise*. They used to come in for breakfast together all the time until Mr. Clemens moved a couple of years ago. He lives in New York now."

While Mary watched from the kitchen and mentally added 'chuckaboos' to her list of slang words, Mr. Clemens and Mr. Wright finished their meal. She hurried to their table, wanting one last opportunity to see the soon-to-be-famous authors before they left.

"Thank you for your patronage!" she said brightly. "That will be thirty cents, please." While she waited for them to pay, she asked, "Are you staying in town, or are you just visiting?"

"Well, I'm just visiting," Mr. Clemens said as he dug around in his pocket, "but seeing as how Mr. Wright lives here, I believe he'll be staying," Smiling, he placed several coins in her hand, and then both men stood up to leave. As they were walking out the door, Mary heard Mr. Clemens say, "The poor thing seems a bit touched in the head."

To which Mr. Wright replied, "Yes, but she did seem eager to please. I hope you gave her a nice tip."

Alex Taylor's Journal – August 31, 1869

Finally! I'm done with mining! School starts on September 13th, and I get to take the whole time off between now and then. Dad and Uncle Bill are going to keep working our claims, which makes me feel a little bit guilty, but at the same time, it's going to be so great to take a break. I'm going to go swimming every day until school starts.

On September 8th there is going to be a baseball game between the Carson City Silver Star Base Ball Club and the Virginia Base Ball Club, which is the name of the Virginia City team, but I don't know if we can go because they are going to play in Carson City. Bill said that baseball is a completely new sport in 1869, and they're still figuring out what the rules will be. That seems so weird to me. I really hope we get to go to the game.

<u>*Natalie Taylor's Journal – August 31, 1869*</u>

I'm so bored. I can't wait for school to start. I'm tired of watching Ben. I'm even getting a little bit bored with swimming, except that I get to hang out with Teddy. I went to the library, but the books are mostly boring stories about being a good girl, or a good boy. I did like Hans Brinker or the Silver Skates, *though. That's a pretty good story, about a boy and his sister who both want to win an ice skating race.*

Yesterday was Alex's last day of working at the mining claims, so maybe it'll be more fun with him around. Plus, school starts pretty soon, which kind of makes me excited, but also means Teddy will be leaving. His family is going to Europe for a while. I think they must have a lot of money, because they travel to Europe all the time, and Teddy told me that he has a governess – which is like a private teacher – and she goes with them everywhere.

Chapter 12

The End of Summer

Alex was determined to make the most of the last few days before school started. He was proud of the work he had done at the mining claim, and he appreciated that his father and Uncle Bill treated him like an adult, but he was ready to spend some time with people who were closer to his own age. As far as he could tell, being an adult meant doing a lot of work, without much time for fun. Until school started, he planned to sleep late every morning, read a bunch of books, and go swimming every afternoon. The only problem was that this was the fourth day in a row that he was awake as soon as the sun rose.

"It's not fair," he grumbled to himself, staring at the ceiling.

He listened as his father and Uncle Bill left for breakfast at the restaurant, and then heard his mother opening the squeaky fire door for the stove. He pushed back his covers and got out of bed without making a sound. His brother and sister were still asleep, so he quietly pulled on his pants and shirt, and then picked up his shoes. He carefully shut the bedroom door behind him and walked barefoot into the kitchen, carrying his shoes.

"Good morning!" his mother said. "I'm making some coffee. Would you like some?"

If they had been back in their own time, Mary would not have offered coffee to her thirteen-year-old son, but it seemed like everyone, including children, drank coffee in Virginia City. Besides, for the last several weeks, Alex had been doing the work of a full-grown adult, and the entire family frequently treated him like one.

"Sure. Thanks, Mom," he said, as he pulled yesterday's socks out of his shoes and started to put them on.

"Are those the same socks you wore yesterday?" she asked.

Alex paused for a moment. There wasn't anything he could do but admit it. After all, she had seen him take them out of his shoes. He finished pulling the sock up, and said, "Yeah, they are."

"Don't you have any clean socks?"

"Yeah, I guess I do," he said, pulling on the other sock, "but they're in the dresser, and I didn't want to wake up Nat and Ben."

"Just tell me you don't make it a habit to wear dirty socks every day," his mother said.

"I don't," he said. "You always told us to make sure we were wearing clean socks and clean underwear so we wouldn't be embarrassed if we got hit by a car or something and had to go to the hospital."

They looked at each other without saying anything. Both of them were thinking about how there weren't any cars around to be worried about. The family was doing the best they could to be happy in 1869, but sometimes all they really wanted was to be back in their own time. Alex tried to think of something to say that would lighten the moment, but nothing seemed right. He finished tying his shoes and said, "If the coffee's ready, I would like to have a cup."

Mary poured two cups. Mother and son sat across the kitchen table from each other, sipping their coffee. After a few minutes, she asked, "So, what are your plans for the day?"

"Well, I *planned* to sleep in," Alex said with a wry smile.

"So much for that plan," his mother said, smiling back at him. "How would you feel about walking down to the *Territorial Enterprise* and picking up a newspaper?"

"Sure. I'll take Pete with me."

From the corner of the kitchen where he lay, Pete's ears perked up when he heard his name. As soon as Alex snapped his fingers, the little dog was right there by his side, wagging his tail.

"What do you say, boy? Do you want to take a walk?" Alex asked.

Pete danced on his hind legs for a few seconds, showing that he was in favor of the idea. Alex reached down and scratched the top of his head.

"OK, boy, let's go," he said, standing up from the table.

Mary smiled, watching them over the rim of her coffee cup. After they left, she got up and checked the fire beneath the burners of the stove, making sure it would be hot enough when she was ready to cook breakfast. Then she checked to see that there was fresh kindling in the oven and moved a few of the pieces around before closing the door. In a couple of hours, she would light that and add a few small pieces of wood. She was going to roast a chicken all by herself today, and she wanted to get the preparations done early.

After a few minutes, Alex and Pete came back with the newspaper. Mary read the first page while Alex played tug-of-war with the dog. When she finished the first page, she handed it to Alex, and then started reading the next page. She was about halfway through that page when Natalie and Benjamin emerged from the bedroom, rubbing their eyes and asking about breakfast.

While her children ate their breakfasts, Mary started gathering the things she would need to prepare dinner. She selected an apple and an onion that would be cut into quarters and stuffed into the chicken, keeping it moist and tender. She checked under the towel that was covering the chicken. It was sitting in a roasting pan packed with ice, to be sure it would stay cold until it was time to start the dinner preparations. Then she cut a length of twine that she would use to tie the legs together when she had finished stuffing it.

She was choosing potatoes from the potato bin when Natalie asked her brothers, "What do you think about heading over to the pond for a morning swim?"

Alex and Benjamin were in complete agreement with the idea and suggested an after-swim picnic, which Mary thought was a wonderful idea. With everybody out of the house, she would be able to focus on her cooking.

Alex wrapped some bread and cheese in pieces of cloth and put them in a basket they could carry to the pond. Mary added three corked bottles of water and three home-made pickles from the batch she had placed in jars and "put up" in the root cellar the week before.

She kissed each of her children on the forehead as they left the house, and then poured herself a second cup of coffee. Setting her coffee on the end table, she sat down on the couch and scratched the top of Pete's head for a minute. Then she settled back to finish reading page two of the Territorial Enterprise. She had at least two hours to herself and she planned to enjoy them.

Since it was so early in the day, there weren't very many people at the pond, but Teddy and his brother Elliott were already there, and they had staked out the best spot under the only tree that was close to the pond. Hoping to share some of the shade, the Taylors offered to share some of their picnic lunch in exchange for a spot under the tree. Teddy and Elliott were happy to take them up on the offer, and they all sat together for a few minutes, chatting. Elliott and Benjamin wandered off a little ways and started digging a fort, while Alex went straight down to the pond and jumped in. Teddy was wearing a bathing suit today, and Natalie asked him about it.

"Are you planning to swim today?"

"I am! I've been getting more exercise, and I'm building up my stamina."

"And you think that will help with your asthma?" Natalie asked.

"I'm sure it will!" he responded. "The more exercise I get, the stronger my lungs are. From now on I plan to get lots of exercise." He took a deep breath and exhaled loudly. "See?" he said.

Natalie nodded. "I'm glad you're feeling better," she said.

Teddy stood up and pounded his chest with his fist.

"I feel great!" he said. "Maybe we can have a race across the pond."

Natalie smiled and said, "You're on! I'll bet you a pickle I can beat you!"

"I don't have any pickles," Teddy said, "but I'll bet nickel against your pickle."

"A nickel and a pickle," Natalie said, laughing. "OK, it's a bet!"

Teddy and Natalie shook hands on it, and when Alex came back to the picnic area, they asked him to serve as the judge.

When they saw there would be a race, Elliott and Benjamin joined Teddy, Alex, and Natalie at the edge of the pond. Teddy and Natalie stood side-by-side at the edge of the pond, poised to dive in.

"On your mark," Alex shouted. "Get set. Go!"

Teddy and Natalie both dove into the water. Elliott and Benjamin shouted encouragement to their siblings, running around to the other side of the pond to see who would win. Alex ran with them, doing his best impression of a sports announcer.

"And it's Natalie out in front, but she'll have to work hard to keep the lead. Here comes Teddy from behind! He's gaining on her. Gaining on her! Teddy takes the lead! Natalie is fighting hard to regain the lead. She's gaining on him. She's taking the lead, but Teddy is kicking hard, and... Natalie is the winner! I repeat, Natalie is the winner!"

Natalie and Teddy climbed out of water at the other end of the pond.

"Double or nothing?" Teddy asked.

"Sure!" Natalie said. "I don't mind taking two of your nickels."

"Ooh, a little trash talking at the starting line," Alex said, smiling.

"Trash...talking?" Teddy said, looking puzzled.

"You know, smacking you down," Alex said.

"I'm afraid you have me at sixes and sevens," Teddy replied.

"Six and seven what?" Alex asked.

"What?" asked Teddy.

"What?" asked Alex.

Natalie clapped her hands together, and said "Boys! Can we get on with the rematch?"

"Oh, yes, of course," Teddy said. "Prepare to be bested!"

"Prepare to be bested?" Natalie asked, but there was no time to get a response.

"On your mark, get set, go!"

Teddy and Natalie were surprised by Alex's quick countdown, and they both went into the water awkwardly—partly diving and partly falling in.

Alex, Benjamin, and Elliott ran to the other side of the pond.

"And it's Natalie in the lead," Alex said, continuing his sports monologue as he ran. "Teddy is kicking hard, but Natalie is pulling away. Teddy is catching up, but, wait, he is falling behind again! Natalie has taken the lead. Natalie is solidly in the lead! Natalie wins!"

Alex had arrived at the other side of the pond, and he reached down to pull Natalie out. He turned to help Teddy next, but Teddy wasn't anywhere to be seen. Elliot was running along the side of the pond, pointing to the water.

"Teddy!" he shouted. "He went under the water!"

"What?" Natalie asked, in a panic. "Do you see him?"

Elliott pointed to a spot near the middle of the pond. "He was there!" he said, with a terrified look on his face. "And then he went under!"

Immediately, Natalie dove back into the water, completely forgetting that she was supposed to strip down to her bloomers and her father's t-shirt if she ever had to rescue somebody. With powerful strokes, she swam towards the bottom of the lake. Her eyes were stinging, but she had to keep them open if she was going to find Teddy. She looked around frantically and finally saw him through the murky water. With one hand, she grabbed the fabric of his bathing suit and pulled him towards her. With her other hand, she reached above her and started swimming straight up to the surface of the pond, kicking with all her might to help propel them both upward.

Looking up, she could see that she was getting close to the surface, but the two swimming races had tired her out, and her lungs felt like they were bursting. The combined weight of Teddy's body and the heavy bathing dress she was wearing were too much for her. She desperately needed air, and she knew she would never make it to the surface while she was holding onto him. Hating herself for doing it, she released her hold on Teddy's bathing suit and shot up through the surface of the pond, gasping.

As soon as Alex saw her come up without Teddy, he dove in to the water and grabbed Teddy's arm before he could sink back down very far. He swam for the surface, pulling Teddy along with him, and then held Teddy's head above water as he swam to the edge of the pond. Elliott and Benjamin were standing there, looking terrified.

A few yards away, Natalie pulled herself out of the pond. Still gasping for breath, she rolled onto the grass and laid there with her chest heaving.

"Help me get him out of the water!" Alex shouted to the boys.

They grabbed and pulled at Teddy's bathing suit, his hair, and his arms. With Alex doing most of the work, the three of them managed to hoist Teddy out of the water and onto the grassy bank. Alex scrambled out of the pond and rolled Teddy onto his back. Off to the side, he could see that Natalie was sitting up, coughing. Satisfied that his sister was safe, he turned his attention back to Teddy.

This was not a CPR manikin, this was an actual person who needed help, and he had to get it right. He turned Teddy's head to the side so the water would drain out of his mouth and willed his mind to be calm.

He repeated the steps for CPR to himself, and then turned Teddy's head back to the center, pinching his nose closed. Placing his mouth over Teddy's, he blew four strong breaths and put his ear down to hear if Teddy was exhaling. He put his hand on the side of Teddy's neck to feel for a pulse and then watched his chest to see if he had started to breathe on his own.

Nothing.

Elliott was hovering over Alex's shoulder, crying.

"What are you doing to my brother?" he wailed.

"He's trying to save him!" Benjamin said, pulling Elliot by the arm to keep him out of Alex's way.

Alex pinched Teddy's nose again. This time he gave him two strong breaths. Then he did thirty chest compressions. Elliott struggled to break free of Benjamin's grip.

"Stop it! Stop it!" Elliott shouted, not understanding what Alex was doing to his brother.

"Hush!" Alex said, pressing his ear against Teddy's chest, listening carefully. Still, nothing. He watched to see if there was any movement at all, but there was none.

A few yards away, Natalie saw what was happening and struggled to her feet. Staggering under the weight of her wet swimming dress, she moved as quickly as she could to help Benjamin. He was holding Elliott's arm with both hands, trying to keep him away from Alex. Both little boys had tears streaming down their cheeks. When she got close enough, Natalie put her arms around both of them and pulled them down onto the grass, next to her.

They sat huddled together and watched as Alex pinched Teddy's nose again, giving him two more strong breaths.

"It's OK," Natalie said several times, trying to reassure herself and the boys at the same time. "He's trying to help him."

Suddenly, Teddy was choking and spitting up water. He was alive!

"Run to the mine and tell somebody what happened!" Alex called out to the boys. "Tell them to bring something we can use to carry Teddy to the hospital."

Elliott and Benjamin jumped to their feet and took off, running. Alex stayed where he was, kneeling next to Teddy, who was struggling to sit up.

Natalie stood up and made her way over to Alex. She knelt down and gave him a hug. Turning to Teddy, she asked, "Are you OK?"

"I think so," Teddy responded. "What happened?"

"I don't know," Natalie said. "Suddenly you were sinking to the bottom of the pond."

"Oh, I remember," Teddy said, after thinking about it for a few seconds. "I could feel my asthma coming on, and I panicked. I should have floated on my back, but I was trying to get to the edge of the pond, and I kept swallowing water."

"I sent Elliott and Benjamin to the mine to get help," Alex said, "so you should just rest until they get here with a stretcher."

"Oh, no," Teddy protested, "I don't need to be carried on a stretcher. I can walk home."

"That doesn't seem like a good idea," Alex said, remembering that his first aid book said people who nearly drown should get immediate medical attention after they are revived.

Teddy stood up and swayed, and then abruptly sat back down. "Maybe I'll just rest for a few minutes," he said.

The three of them sat on the grass, each engrossed in his own thoughts, until they heard several people approaching. Two men were running towards them, and one was carrying a stretcher. Elliott and Benjamin were right behind them.

"Which one of you needs the stretcher?" asked the first man. Alex and Natalie both pointed at Teddy.

"I don't need a stretcher," Teddy insisted. "I'll be all right in a minute. I can walk home."

The men looked at him doubtfully, and then looked back at Alex and Natalie, who both shrugged.

169

"Well, OK," said the man, "but we'll wait here for a couple of minutes to make sure you're all right."

Teddy stood up again, this time with more success. "See?" he said. "I'm OK."

"We'll walk home with him," Alex volunteered. "Thank you for coming here so quickly, but I guess we can't make him get on the stretcher."

The men turned away and headed back to the mine. "These dang kids," one of them said, shaking his head.

"I'm surprised none of them have actually drowned yet," said the other.

Natalie stood up and wrung out the hem of her skirt. "I guess we should start heading to Teddy's house," she said.

"I don't need everybody to walk with me," Teddy said.

"Which one of us do you think wants to stay here and swim?" asked Natalie.

Teddy nodded his head and resigned himself to the company of all four of them on his walk home. "We don't have to mention this to anybody," he said. "It would just worry my parents unnecessarily, and you can see that I'm fine now."

"No deal, bro," said Alex. "Your parents definitely need to know so they can take care of you if you get sick or something from inhaling all that pond water."

"Bro?" Teddy asked, trying to change the subject, but also wondering about some of the strange expressions the Alex, Natalie and Benjamin used.

"Bro. Brother. You know, like, you're my brother. You're a guy, and you're my friend," Alex explained.

"Oh." Teddy said. "You know, sometimes I don't know what the Sam Hill you are saying."

"The feeling is mutual," Alex said, smiling.

When they arrived at Teddy's house, Alex didn't need to tell anyone about the incident at the pond. Elliott opened the door and ran in shouting, "Mother! Father! Teddy almost drowned!"

Alex turned to his brother and sister and said, "I think our work here is done."

"So do I," said Natalie.

"Me, too," said Benjamin. They all stepped back from the door and headed for home.

When they got back to their house, they told Mary what had happened at the pond. She stopped peeling potatoes and gave each of her children a hug.

"I am so proud of you," she said, "and so glad that you're all safe, and Teddy is safe. Go change out of your wet bathing suits. I think a quiet afternoon is in order after all that excitement."

That evening, Mary served the chicken she had roasted with mashed potatoes and green beans. Everyone agreed that it was delicious, and nobody left the table until all the food was gone. Then Alex, Natalie, and Benjamin told their story about Teddy at the pond again. Their father and Uncle Bill were impressed with their quick action and determination to save their friend.

After dinner, they were cleaning up the kitchen when someone knocked at their front door. Thomas went to answer it, and after a few seconds, he called for everyone to join him. Curious, they stopped what they were doing, taking turns drying their hands on the dishtowel.

When they got to the front door, they saw a man and woman they hadn't ever met before, but the Taylor children all recognized Teddy, who was standing between them.

"Hi, Teddy," Natalie said.

"We don't want to disturb your evening," the man said, "but we felt compelled to come and tell you how grateful we are to your children for their actions today at the pond."

"Won't you come in?" Mary invited them.

"We can only stay for a few minutes," said the woman, stepping over the threshold, "but thank you." The man and boy followed her into the house. "My name is Margaret, and this is my husband, Cornelius."

"My name is Mary, and this is my husband, Thomas. And I take it that you are Teddy," Mary

172

said, addressing the boy who was standing between the two adults.

"Yes, ma'am," Teddy said, extending his hand. "I'm Teddy. Teddy Roosevelt."

"Did you say…" Mary faltered.

"Teddy Roosevelt?" Thomas said, shaking Teddy's hand while he completed Mary's question.

"Yes, sir, yes, ma'am," Teddy said, politely.

Thomas, Mary, Alex, Natalie, and Bill stood there blinking. They were all thinking the same thing. *Teddy Roosevelt is going to be the President of the United States one day!*

Bill was the first to recover.

"It's nice to meet you, Teddy," he said.

Mrs. Roosevelt reached for Mary's hand and held it for a moment. "From one mother's heart to another," she said, "thank you for raising such wonderful, caring children. Elliott told us how each of your children had a role in rescuing Teddy. The way Elliott described it, things looked desperate for a few minutes, but, fortunately, everything turned out all right in the end. We couldn't be more grateful, even if the way they handled the situation was…. somewhat…." She paused, searching for the right word.

Mr. Roosevelt cleared his throat and said, "Unconventional."

"Yes, unconventional," Mrs. Roosevelt said. She released Mary's hand and shook hands with each of the Taylor children, one at a time, saying "thank you," to each one.

"We're leaving Virginia City tomorrow, but we didn't want to go without expressing our thanks," Mr. Roosevelt said.

"Yes, thank you for everything," Teddy said. "I'm very glad I got to meet all of you." He reached into his pocket and held out two nickels to Natalie. "I believe I owe you these."

Natalie took the nickels and asked, "Are you sure?"

"Oh, definitely," Teddy replied. "That's probably the best ten cents I will ever spend in my whole life."

Natalie closed her fingers around the nickels and smiled.

"Goodbye," she said. "I'll miss you, but I hope you have a good time in Europe!"

"Goodbye," Teddy said. "And thank you. I hope we come back to Virginia City again, soon."

"Yes, thank you," Mr. Roosevelt echoed. "And good night. We will include you in our prayers."

"Yes, we will," Mrs. Roosevelt said, nodding.

"Good night to you, too," Mary said, as Thomas opened the door for them. "And God bless."

After the Roosevelts left, Thomas closed the door, and everyone stood there staring at it for a minute. Alex finally broke the silence.

"Teddy Roosevelt!" he said. "Teddy Freaking Roosevelt!"

"Teddy Freaking Roosevelt!" echoed Natalie.

"Teddy Freaking Roosevelt!" said Benjamin.

"Do you even know who Teddy Roosevelt is?" Alex asked.

"No, not really," Benjamin said, making the rest of the family laugh.

They spent the rest of the evening talking about the people they had met since arriving in 1869, and how amazing it was to talk to people they had only read about in their history books before they took their accidental journey through time.

The conversation was still going on when Bill left for his regular visit with Caroline, and he was sure it would continue for most of the evening. With all the talk about time travel, he decided this might not be a good evening to bring her to the house, so he invited her to take an evening stroll with him instead.

They walked together in the moonlight, not noticing the passage of time, pausing several times to exchange romantic kisses. When they parted that night, both of them wondered if they might be falling in love.

Chapter 13

School Days

"Aren't you excited?" Mary asked. "The first day of school is always an adventure, and you'll make lots of new friends."

"I'm guessing they don't have a swim team," Natalie said. "Even if they did, I guess the girls' team would be called 'The Beached Whales' considering what the bathing suits are like."

"It's easy to spot the negative things in life." Mary said, "What are the positives?"

"I don't know," Natalie replied. "Maybe you should ask me after school, instead of right now."

"Well, keep an eye out for the positives. I'm looking forward to hearing all about your first day!"

Mary turned to Benjamin and gave him a kiss on the forehead.

"And it's your first day in first grade! How do you feel?"

"I'm fine," he answered. "Did you put an apple in my lunch?"

"Yes, I did, and it's cut into quarters, the way you like it."

Benjamin nodded, with a serious expression on his face. "Then I think I'm ready to go," he said.

Mary turned to her oldest child and said, "Alex, look after your sister and brother, OK?"

"I don't need looking after!" Natalie protested.

"Well, then, both of you, look out for your little brother." She stepped back to get a better look at them and said, "Oh, I wish I could get a picture."

She handed each of her children a lunch pail and gave them a peck on the cheek.

"School is dismissed at 3:30, so I'll expect you to be home by 4:00, OK?"

All three of the children nodded and then headed out the front door. As soon as the door closed behind them, Mary went to the front window so she could watch them as they left. When they finally disappeared from sight, she took a deep breath and started clearing away the breakfast dishes. She needed to use the kitchen table to cut out a pattern for a new apron, and Caroline was coming over soon to help her learn how to use the new foot-pedal–operated sewing machine she had purchased the week before.

While Mary washed the breakfast dishes, her children walked down Flowery Street and past the Mackay Mansion, towards the Third Ward School. Along the way, Natalie filled Alex in on the details she had learned over the summer about the town and its inhabitants.

"That's the Savage Mine Office," Natalie said, pointing to a large building to their left as they walked along D Street. "And that's where John Mackay lives," she continued, pointing out the big two-story brick house a little further down the road on the right. "He's super-rich. Everybody in town really likes him. I've never seen him, but I've heard he's very nice. He buys tickets for the children who want to see performances at Piper's Opera House but can't afford to go. He has a step-daughter named Eva. She's my age, but she doesn't go to regular school. I think she has a governess, like Teddy."

As they got closer to the school, they started encountering other children who were headed the same way.

"Hello, I'm Gertrude," said a little girl with blonde hair, who had hurried to catch up with them. "I'm in third grade. What grade are you in?"

Natalie answered for all of them, "My little brother, Ben, is in first grade, and my older brother, Alex, is in eighth grade. I'm Natalie, and I'm in seventh grade."

"Oh, then none of you will be in my class," Gertrude said. "I've never seen you before, so you must be new. We get a lot of new people here all the time."

"Yes," Natalie replied, "We're new."

"Oh," Gertrude said, walking faster so she could catch up to the next group of children ahead of them. "Well, goodbye! It was nice to meet you."

They could hear her introducing herself when she reached the next group.

"Well, *she's* very friendly." Natalie said. "I hope she finds somebody in the third grade before she gets all the way to school."

They continued walking, calling out greetings to everyone they saw. By the time they reached the front doors of the school, they had spoken to so many people along the way they couldn't remember most of their names.

Knowing they were about to go into different classrooms, they stopped for a minute before entering the building.

"Meet you back here at lunch time?" Natalie asked.

"Sure," Alex said casually, as though he wasn't nervous at all.

"Sure," said Benjamin, imitating his big brother. He offered a fist-bump to his sister.

"Pow!" she said, opening her hand wide after the bump. "OK, here goes nothing!"

She took a deep breath and led the way through the front doors of the school. There was a lady sitting at a desk in the hallway, and she found Natalie's name on a list. After she directed Natalie to her classroom, she turned to Alex and Benjamin. Alex gave the lady their names, and they waited to see where they were supposed to go.

"I'm glad to see you helping your little brother," she said to Alex. "Benjamin Taylor, I see you are an Abcedarian! You will go to Classroom 1."

"Excuse me," Alex asked, "what's an Abcedarian?"

"That is what we call our youngest students," the lady replied. "Because they are learning their ABCs."

"Oh," Alex said, "OK."

"And you, young man," she said to Alex, "will go to Classroom 5, which is upstairs."

Alex walked Benjamin to his classroom and left him at the door with a reminder.

"When we go outside today, Natalie and I will meet you near the front doors, so look for us by the doors at lunchtime, OK? If we aren't there yet, just wait by the doors and we'll find you. Got it?"

Benjamin nodded. "Got it," he said, looking a little fearful. "Should I tell the teacher I can't be an Abcedarian, because I already know my ABCs?"

Alex laughed, and said, "I don't think you need to worry about that. It'll be fine, Ben. I'll see you later."

With that, Alex turned and headed for the steps that led to his classroom upstairs. "It'll be fine," he repeated to himself quietly.

All three of the Taylors were surprised when they entered their classrooms. Classes at this school were separated by gender, so everyone in Natalie's class was a girl, while Alex and Benjamin's classes only had boys.

So much for Sarah being in my class, Alex thought. He would have to wait until the lunch recess to see if she attended the Third Ward School at all.

"Good morning, class," said his teacher. "My name is Mr. White. Welcome to the eighth grade. I will begin by reminding you of the school's daily schedule." He turned and pointed to the chalkboard at the front of the class. "I expect my students to adhere to this schedule. Let us begin."

In Natalie's classroom and Benjamin's classroom, very similar orientations were taking place, except that Natalie's day also included "Needlework and Other Domestic Skills" as a subject. Her teacher was Miss Matthews, and Benjamin's teacher was Miss Bisbie. Both teachers had also written the daily schedule on the chalkboard at the front of their classrooms, but the one in Benjamin's classroom was written in block letters.

Benjamin stared at the chalkboard with wide eyes. He did know his alphabet, and he had learned to sound out a few words, but there weren't very many words that he could actually read by himself. He knew the schedule on the chalkboard was important, but he didn't know what it said. He could feel his stomach doing flips. He raised his hand, and Miss Bisbie nodded at him.

"Yes? You, there, with your hand up. What is your name?"

"Benjamin Taylor," Benjamin said.

"Yes, Benjamin, what is it?" she asked.

"I can't read the schedule you wrote on the board."

"Really?" the teacher asked, looking surprised. "How many students do I have that in this class who cannot read the schedule? Raise your hands, please."

Almost every student in the class raised his hand, and Miss Bisbie put her hand up to her chin as she surveyed the room.

"Well, I think you are all wrong," she said. "As long as you know the alphabet, you can read. It's just that your brains might not know that yet. Let's start with this word here, on the first line." She pointed to the word "Bell." "Who can tell me what sound the first letter in this word makes?" Every student raised his hand. "Oh, my," she said, "everyone knows what sound this letter makes! Let's say it together. One, two, three!"

In unison, the entire class said, "buh." Miss Bisbie smiled, and Benjamin felt his stomach settle back down where it was supposed to be. First grade might be all right, after all.

When the lunch bell rang at 11:50, Alex, Natalie, and Benjamin met near the front doors of the school, as they had planned.

"Well," Alex asked Benjamin, "what do you think?"

"I like my teacher. Her name is Miss Bisbie," he said.

"That's a good start," Alex said. "I'm not too sure about my teacher."

"Why?" Natalie asked. "Mine seems like she's OK."

"My teacher is Mr. White, and he seems very strict. It will probably be OK, but he's kind of like a robot." In a monotone voice, Alex imitated his teacher, "It is now 9:50 and we will commence with Grammar."

"Eww," said Natalie. "I hope he isn't like that all the time. Maybe he's just nervous because it's the first day of school."

"He seems pretty old. I don't think he's a new teacher, so he's probably not nervous," Alex said, craning his neck around to survey the crowded schoolyard, "but we'll see. Maybe he'll loosen up later on."

"What are you looking for?" Natalie asked.

"Nothing," Alex said. "Just a place where we can eat lunch."

"No, you weren't," Natalie said, teasing him. "You were looking for Sarah. Did you see her?"

"Not yet," Alex admitted, "but people are still coming out of the building, so maybe she'll be here pretty soon. If she even goes to school here," he added, attempting to sound casual.

"Did you guys notice?" Natalie asked, changing the subject, "there's no Pledge of Allegiance."

Alex stopped scanning the schoolyard and looked at his sister. "You're right!" he said. "I wonder when the pledge was invented?"

Natalie shrugged and said, "I don't know, but it seems like it hasn't been invented yet. It just felt a little strange. Not saying it, I mean."

"Yeah, it does seem a little strange, now that you mention it." Alex said.

Just then, Sarah walked out of the school building. She was talking with two other girls as she descended the front steps. Alex stood and watched her without speaking.

"So, she does go to school here!" Natalie exclaimed triumphantly.

"Shh!" Alex said, "I don't want her to think I'm a total doof."

"No problem," Natalie said, lowering her voice. "I'm gonna go sit on that log over there and eat my lunch. Come on, Benjamin. Let's give Alex some space so he can gawk at the pretty girls, and not have to worry about his siblings making him look like a doof."

She turned and headed towards the log. Benjamin hung back for a few seconds.

"Hey, you should stop staring at her like that if you don't want her to think you're a doof," he said.

Alex's eyes shifted quickly away from Sarah, and focused on his little brother, who was casually strolling away, holding up his hand to show that he was snapping his fingers.

"Oh, snap," Alex muttered, embarrassed that Benjamin seemed to be the cool one right now. He looked back at Sarah and saw that she was talking with a group of girls. She seemed to be having fun, so he decided he would wait for another day before he tried to talk to her. He walked in the direction of his brother and sister, hoping they would let him eat lunch with them, and trying to decide whether or not he owed them an apology.

That afternoon, when the bell rang at 3:30, the Taylor children met at the front doors of the school, as they had planned, and walked home together. Benjamin talked non-stop, the whole way about his teacher and his classmates, his desk, his slate, the way the chalk kind of crumbled at the end when he wrote on the slate, and every other topic that came into his mind. Alex and Natalie were both preoccupied with their own thoughts about their first day at school in 1869, so they were perfectly happy to let him ramble on while they walked.

At dinner that night, the first day of school continued to be the big topic.

"My teacher said he requires all of his students to take turns chopping kindling and bringing in the wood for the stove in the classroom," Alex said. "When it's your turn, you have to get there early so he can start the fire before the school day starts. Can he make us do that?"

Before anyone could respond, Natalie said, "My teacher didn't say anything about that, but maybe the boys take care of the wood for all the classrooms. The girls take turns being the Ink Monitor. That's the person who puts ink in those little holes on top of the desks."

"Hey, I was asking a question," Alex said.

"Oh, sorry, was that a real question?"

Before Alex could get an answer, Benjamin reached for his glass of milk and said, "We're learning a poem. Next week we have to take turns saying the whole poem to the class. It goes: 'I've grown so big, I go to school.' There's more, but I can't remember it right now." He took a long drink and came up with a milk mustache, gasping for air. "And write upon a slate!" he exclaimed. "That's the next line in the poem!"

Thomas looked at Mary and smiled.

"Just embracing the moment," he said, "before we have to give this day back to the space-time continuum."

I've grown so big, I go to school,
And write upon a slate,
And say now, two and two make four,
And four and four make eight.

Chapter 14

Base Ball

"Some guys at school were talking about baseball today," Alex said after dinner a few days later. "There's a Virginia City team, and a team in Carson City. They're going to play their first game against each other next Saturday. Do you think we can go?"

"Where are they playing?" Thomas asked.

"It's in Carson City," Alex answered.

Bill looked up from the book he was reading, and said, "I'd like to go, and maybe take Caroline. We could pack a picnic lunch and rent a six-person carriage from the livery down the street."

"I think I saw something in the newspaper about it," Mary said, thumbing through that day's *Territorial Enterprise*. "Here it is!"

She re-read the article to herself and smiled. "That's great!" she said. "They're going to fence off the playing field to protect the players from wandering cattle."

"I saw that article earlier," Alex said. "Did you notice that 'baseball' is two words? Base ball."

"It sounds like it might be fun," Thomas said. "Does everybody want to go to the baseball game in Carson City this Saturday?"

All the Taylors said yes. Bill said yes, too, but he had to check with Caroline before he could say for sure that she would go with them.

"We should probably go check the livery stables right now to see if we can rent a carriage," Bill said. "Other people are going to have the same idea, and there may not be very many six-person carriages available."

"Good idea," said Thomas. "I'll do that now, while you check with Caroline to see if she wants to go with us."

Both men headed out the front door. Alex turned to Benjamin and smiled. "Cool!"

Benjamin held up his palm for a high-five and smiled back at him. "Yeah, cool!" he said, as Alex's palm smacked into his.

"How is it you know how to handle a carriage like this?" Thomas asked Bill, as they traveled down Devil's Gate Toll Road towards Carson City. It was a beautiful Saturday morning, and Thomas's quick trip to the livery stable the week before had been successful. Having six passenger seats gave them more than enough room, and the leather straps that held the seats in place absorbed some of the bumps in the road.

Bill and Caroline were sitting at the front of the wagon, and Bill was holding the reins, encouraging the horses to keep a steady pace.

"I paid one of the stable hands at the livery to give me a couple of lessons!" Bill replied, smiling. "I'd never driven a carriage like this before last Tuesday."

"I'm impressed," Thomas said.

"Well, I can recommend young Mr. O'Hara at the Spaulding & Gearhart Livery Stable, if you want to learn. He was an excellent teacher. I'm sure it helps that we stay on the same road most of the way to Carson City. The horses don't seem to need a lot of direction."

Caroline wondered how it was that neither of these full-grown men had ever driven a carriage before. She was about to ask when Mary spoke.

"We couldn't have asked for a nicer day. Not a cloud in the sky and the temperature is perfect."

"It should be a fun day," Thomas said, "although it won't be quite the same without hotdogs."

Confused, Caroline turned in her seat and looked at Thomas over her shoulder. "Hot dogs?" she asked. "You wanted to bring dogs with us to the game?"

"Uh, well, no, uh, but yes, but no," Thomas stuttered. Sometimes he forgot Caroline was not from their time. He would have to be more careful about that. His mind raced through his possible answers. Frankfurters? Were those a 'thing' in 1869? There was no way to be sure.

"I guess I was just thinking about the way dogs pant when they get hot," he said lamely.

Caroline was even more puzzled than she was a minute ago, but she didn't say anything. She turned back towards the front of the carriage and watched Bill for a while. He stared straight ahead without speaking. He couldn't think of anything that would help Thomas out of his awkward moment.

Meanwhile, Caroline was thinking about the strange words and phrases she kept hearing from this family. Like *'noob'* and *'google,'* and *'superhero.'* It was as though they had their own version of the English language. Some of the words sounded familiar, but the meaning was somehow different. Every time she figured out what a word meant, she felt like she was one step closer to becoming a member of their secret club, but it was very confusing.

When they got close to the playing field in Carson City, they could see that this ball game was going to be a very big event. There were already at least a hundred people setting up picnic areas around the playing field, and behind them, at least fifty more carriages and wagons were making their way to the field.

"Where should we park?" Alex asked.

"I don't think it matters too much, but it looks like there's more space along the third baseline," Bill said.

"Oh, good, since we're the visiting team, that's perfect," Alex said.

For a moment, Caroline wondered why Alex seemed to think that the third baseline was where visitors should sit. Then she saw a good place to park the carriage and pointed to a tree that was set back a little further from the field.

"We could go over there," she said. "It's not as close, but there's a little hill there, and we'd have some nice shade."

"Sounds good to me," Bill said, pulling the reins in that direction. "Thank you, boys," he said, when they arrived at the designated spot.

"Did you just thank the horses?" Caroline asked.

"Yep!" Bill responded, smiling. "I sure did."

Caroline smiled back at him and then climbed down and started unloading the blankets and baskets. She thought Bill was one of the most unusual men she had ever met, but in a good way. She let herself hope they might have a future together.

With everyone helping, it wasn't long before they had set up their picnic site. They spread the blankets along one side of the carriage so they could take advantage of the additional shade it provided, and then set out the containers of food. Mary had packed cold fried chicken, hard-boiled eggs, a block of cheese, two loaves of bread, and a dozen apples. Caroline brought a basket packed with plates and silverware, a pie from the restaurant, and a jug of lemonade.

As the baseball players started arriving, the Taylor group settled themselves on the blankets and passed their food back and forth.

"Ah, this is the life," Bill said, leaning back against one of the wagon wheels as he bit into a chicken drumstick.

"Yes, it is," Thomas agreed, taking a bite from a hard-boiled egg.

Once again, Mary wished she could take a picture, and it occurred to her she might have to learn how to draw, or paint, if she wanted to capture any of these moments with her family.

When they finished eating, Benjamin occupied himself by tying long blades of grass together, while Alex and Natalie opened a deck of cards and played a game of Crazy Eights. The adults positioned themselves to take advantage of the backrests provided by the carriage wheels, and Caroline sat with her head resting on Bill's shoulder.

Thomas was the only one paying attention to the ball field, so everyone was surprised when he asked, "What are they wearing?"

"What?" asked Mary.

"Look at their pants," Thomas said in a puzzled voice.

"Whose pants?" Caroline asked.

"The Virginia City players are wearing long pants. That's going to slow them down."

"Is that a problem?"

"It might be. It seems like a small thing, but sometimes a little thing like that can make a big difference. The Carson City team is wearing short pants with long socks, so it will be easier for them to run."

Caroline looked at the Virginia City team's pants with increased interest. "I see what you mean," she said, and then turned to Bill with a *"who knew?"* look on her face.

"I think they're getting started," Alex said. "I have a list of the players here. I cut it out of the newspaper this morning,"

"Here we go!" he continued, "Ladies and gentlemen, welcome to the Carson City Plaza Field, in Carson City, Nevada, for today's match-up between the Virginia City Base Ball Club and the Carson City Silver Stars. Leading off for the Carson City Silver Stars, and playing the defensive position of catcher is," he peered at the newspaper article, "Bergesser—wait a minute. Is that Bergesser?"

"They don't have names or numbers on their shirts," Thomas observed.

"That's going to make it a little tough to call the game," Alex said.

"Who is this guy?" Thomas asked. "The one walking out to the middle of the field. He has a cane."

Bill sat up and squinted so he could see the man better. "He has a top hat," he said in amazement.

Standing near the pitcher, the man began shouting to the crowd.

"Ladies and gentlemen, your attention is directed to the rules of the game. No profanity is allowed. No booing is allowed. The game will be conducted in a gentlemanly and orderly manner. The ball must be thrown to the batter in a gentlemanly way. A strike is called if the batter swings and misses. Three strikes, and the batter is out. A ball is called if the pitch is not hittable. If the batter receives six balls, they may walk freely to first base."

After delivering this information, the man turned around and walked back to home plate, where he took his position standing behind the catcher.

"He must be the umpire," Bill said. All the Taylors nodded their heads.

"Did he say six balls was a walk?" Natalie asked.

"That's what he said," Thomas answered.

Caroline watched her companions with interest as the game got underway. She was less interested in the actual ballgame.

"Wait, is he pitching underhanded?" asked Alex.

"Looks like it," answered his father.

"Nobody has a glove," Benjamin noted.

"You're right!" said Mary. "It must hurt like the dickens when they catch the ball."

"Not to mention the risk of a few broken fingers. At the least, some serious bruising," Thomas said.

"Does that bat look really long to you?" Bill asked.

"Yeah, it does," said Thomas. "Definitely. That's a very long bat."

Caroline's head turned back and forth as she followed the conversation. "It sounds like all of you have been to see other baseball games," she said.

They stopped talking and looked at her. Then they looked at each other.

"We saw a few games in San Francisco," Bill said weakly.

Caroline thought about that for a few minutes. Why wouldn't they have mentioned that before now? That seemed odd.

For the Taylor family, the game they were watching looked something like baseball, but also like something else. Besides having to pitch underhanded, no curveballs or other kinds of "trick" balls were allowed. The umpire would never call a strike unless the batter actually swung at the ball and missed, and if the batter decided not to swing at a pitch, it was automatically called a ball.

The Carson City Silver Stars were first up to bat, and their first player hit a single to first base. The next two Carson City batters struck out, and the Taylors settled in for an interesting game. Carson City's fourth batter up hit a single to first, and then the Virginia City right fielder overthrew the ball to first base when the fifth batter also hit a single. Two Carson City players made it around the diamond and came home on that error.

"It's OK," Bill said to Caroline. "The Carson City club has two outs. We just need one more out, and then Virginia City gets up to bat."

Fifteen more Carson City players went to bat before the third out was finally called. At the bottom of the first inning, the score was 14–0.

"Well," Thomas said, "that was a rough start, but our guys are up to bat now." He rubbed his hands together in anticipation, and then watched as three consecutive Virginia City players quickly struck out.

"That was fast," he said.

The second and third innings were equally dismal for Virginia City, but they managed to score five runs during the fourth inning, making the score 27–5. Carson City's huge lead was beginning to look insurmountable, though, and by the top of the seventh inning, the score was Carson City 61, Virginia City 25.

After two more painful innings, the Carson City club declared victory. The final score was 82–31.

"82 to 31. Wow. I probably wouldn't have believed it if I hadn't seen it myself," Alex said.

"I thought it was a lot of fun," said Caroline, as they started picking up the remains of their picnic and stowing the baskets in the carriage.

"Yes, it was," Mary agreed, "even though we got clobbered." She looked around, and asked, "Where's Benjamin?"

"He's right over there, Mom."

Natalie pointed to a spot close to the playing field. "He wanted to get a closer look."

Thomas called for Benjamin and motioned for him to come back to the carriage. The adults couldn't help but smile as they watched him running towards them, in his happy skipping, galloping sort of way, his arms flailing as he ran.

"I wish I had that much energy," Bill said.

"And that much joy!" Caroline added.

Benjamin was shouting something as he ran. At first, they couldn't tell what he was saying, but when he got closer, they were able to make it out.

"Rematch! Rematch!" he said, running up to the carriage and slapping the side of it, like it was "home base" in a game of tag. "October 9th!" he said. "They're gonna have a rematch on October 9th. In Virginia City."

"That's next Saturday," said Alex, turning to his father. "Can we go?"

Thomas glanced at Mary to make sure she agreed, and said, "Absolutely!"

"Can I invite Sarah to come with us?" Alex asked.

"Ooh, Sarah," Benjamin said. Alex ignored him and stayed focused on what his parents would say.

"That's fine with me," Thomas answered, "but check with your mother."

"Well," Mary said, while she folded the blankets, "you have to remember that her parents don't know us, and even if we were introduced, they would still want her to be chaperoned. I'm sorry, sweetheart, it would be fine with us, but I really doubt that her parents would let her come."

Alex's face shifted from hopeful, to confused, to dejected, in less than fifteen seconds.

"You mean, I'll never be able to invite her to go anywhere with me?" he asked.

"You can invite her, but her parents probably won't ever give their permission," Mary said. "I know that's not what you want to hear, but that's just the way things are."

She glanced over at Caroline and saw that she was standing close enough to hear their entire conversation. "We can talk about it some more, later," she told him, handing him one of the folded blankets. "Will you help me put these in the carriage?"

Chapter 15

October Arrives

By October, the novelty of going to school in 1869 had worn off. Benjamin was the only Taylor who was still enjoying it, even though he had to remember extra hard to not talk about screens. He had slipped up earlier in the school year and said something to his class about watching a TV show, and now his classmates and his teacher thought there was a place called *The Teevee Theater* in San Francisco.

On the other hand, he had made friends with most of the boys in his class, including Yancy's cousin, Karl, who had finally cleared up the mystery of Yancy's missing toe.

"He was born without his pinky toe," Karl told him.

"That's it?" Benjamin asked, disappointed. "I thought it got chopped off, or maybe a horse stepped on it, or something."

"Nope," Karl said, "my father doesn't have a pinky toe, either, so I think it runs in the family."

"Really?" Benjamin said, giving some thought to this new piece of information, "I never knew anybody who was born without a toe before."

"That's nothing," Karl said. "I saw a two-headed lamb at the circus last year."

"No way!" Benjamin exclaimed. "Was it walking around?"

"Yeah, it walked around," Karl answered. He described the lamb in detail and told Benjamin about other strange animals he had seen at the circus. By the end of the day, he and Benjamin were best friends.

Natalie also made a few friends in her class, but things were different for girls in 1869 and she was more than ready to break free when December 26th arrived. The minute they got back to their own time, she planned to shave the sides of her head and put on some shorts and a tank top. In the meantime, she kept her thoughts about the role of women in 1869 to herself, and tried not to fall asleep while she was supposed to be learning 'Needlework and Other Domestic Skills.'

Alex was conflicted about school. Mr. White was still as strict as he had been on the first day of school, and Alex watched as his classmates were punished for minor things like dropping a pen on the floor or letting a giggle slip out during class. When a rule was broken, Mr. White required the offending student to spend half of his lunch recess sitting in the corner, wearing a big cone-shaped hat called a "dunce cap" on his head.

Alex did his best to stay out of trouble. He wanted his whole lunch recess for himself. In fact, lunch recess was the best part of the day, now that he was spending it with Sarah. They met at the front doors of the school every day at noon, and walked across the schoolyard to an area that had a few small logs they could sit on while they had lunch together.

As his mother had predicted, Sarah wasn't able to come to the baseball game with him on October 9th. "But I know we are going to the Grand Promenade Ball next month," she said. "Will you be there, too?"

"Yes!" Alex answered, happily. "My folks were talking about it the other day. We'll be there, too."

Sarah smiled, and Alex felt his heart beating faster. "Maybe I can introduce you to my parents while we're at the ball," she said.

"Sure," Alex said, wondering if there was something he should know about being introduced to a girl's parents. He made a mental note to check with Caroline about that.

Even though Sarah couldn't go to the next baseball game with him, Alex was still looking forward to it. There had been a lot of conversation at school, and in town, about what had gone wrong with the last game. Most people thought the Virginia City Club had enjoyed themselves too much before the game started. They had been given a warm welcome in Carson City and consumed far too many free beers before the game started.

A plan was already in place to return the favor, and to welcome the Carson City Silver Stars to Virginia City in grand style. With any luck, the Silver Stars would take advantage of the hospitality, and this time, they would be the team at a disadvantage.

On game day, the Taylors once again packed a picnic lunch, but this time they could walk to the game, since it was being held in Virginia City, at the bottom of Union Street.

They settled down on their picnic blankets with high hopes for a Virginia City win, but the Carson City club scored six quick runs in the first inning and then six more in each of the second and third innings, while Virginia City only scored five. At the beginning of the fourth inning, the score was Carson City 18 to Virginia City 5. Except in the eighth inning, the Carson City club outscored Virginia City every time they went up to bat.

The final score was Carson City 54 to Virginia City 17. It had been a lopsided game, but that didn't stop the town from celebrating when it was over. People and players from both cities bought food and drinks for each other in town, and the festivity continued until the early hours of the next morning.

For the rest of the month, baseball games were played between various Nevada clubs all over the state. Baseball was becoming quite popular, and it seemed that the season was going to continue indefinitely. Several games were scheduled to be played in November.

"It just doesn't seem right," Bill said, lowering the newspaper he was reading on a late-October evening. "I think I've adapted pretty well to the things that are different in 1869, but baseball is supposed to be a summer game. I don't see how it can be played in the snow!"

"I agree with you," Thomas said. "Playing in weather like this is ridiculous. There are hardly any spectators anymore. I really wonder what they're thinking."

"I suppose we should remember that baseball is a new sport for these folks. It's going to take a few decades to perfect the game," Bill said, folding the newspaper before setting it on a side table.

"If you and Mary have a few minutes, I've been thinking about our plans for December 26th, and I'd like to talk to you about it."

"Sure," Thomas said, "Let me ask her to join us."

A minute later, he came back into the living with Mary. She was drying her hands on a towel. "What's up?" she asked, taking a seat on the padded rocking chair she had found on sale the week before.

"We're only nine weeks away from December 26th," Bill said, "and I've been thinking about how to get everybody back in the mine."

"So, you have a plan?" Thomas asked.

"I've been reading the production reports in the newspaper for the last few weeks, trying to calculate how much the mine earns in an average hour. I'm thinking we should offer to pay the superintendent enough money to shut down production for thirty minutes on December 26th."

"How much do you think that would take?" Mary asked.

"Seven ounces of gold would to make up for thirty minutes of lost production," Bill said. "I'm thinking we would offer eight ounces, so it sweetens the pot a bit."

"And we already have more than enough gold to do that, right?" Mary asked.

"Oh, definitely," Bill answered. "Wait here a minute," he said, standing up from the couch and heading towards his bedroom.

"I know Thomas has a pretty good idea about how much small gold we've mined," he called out to them, as he disappeared through the doorway, "but, of course, we've traded some of that in for cash over the last few months."

Thomas and Mary waited, listening to him opening and shutting dresser drawers. A minute later, he came out holding two five-pound flour sacks— one in each hand. He set one sack in Thomas' lap and said, "That one is about two-thirds full of nuggets."

He set the other one in Mary's lap and said, "That one is about a halfway full of small gold."

Thomas and Mary looked at each other for a moment before opening the sacks they had been given.

"Oh, my!" Mary said, as she peered into the bag in her lap. "It's very impressive when you see that much gold in one place."

"Holy cow!" Thomas said, looking into his.

They both looked up at Bill, and Thomas asked, "How much do you think all of this is worth?"

"That depends on the year," Bill said. "Right now, in 1869, the small gold in that sack is worth a little more than $1,000. In our time, though, it's worth almost $110,000."

Mary's eyebrows shot up, but she didn't say anything.

"As far as the nuggets go," Bill continued, "if we just go by the weight, they're probably worth around $125,000 in our time—but nuggets are always worth more than small gold. It's hard to say how much more we could get for them. I'm not going to be too far off if I say we have at least $175,000 worth of nuggets. Maybe more."

Thomas did the math in his head. "So, you're saying that we have at least a $285,000 in gold? In our time, I mean." he said. "And maybe more?"

"Right," Bill nodded, "but we still have another nine weeks of mining we can do, and we're doing a lot better now than we were when we first started.

We could have at least $500,000 worth of gold by December 26th."

"Wow!" Thomas said, "Half a million dollars. That's amazing!"

"We've never talked about how to split it up," Bill said, "but I was thinking we take eight ounces out for the mine superintendent and then we split the rest 60/40. You and Mary take 60 percent, and I'll take 40 percent."

"Why wouldn't we split it 50/50?" Mary asked.

"Well, Alex did a lot of mining work," Bill said. "There were two Taylors and just one Johnson, working the claims every day in July and August. For another thing, you've been working hard to take care of the house and the cooking, Mary. I just think it's fair that your family should take 60 percent."

"I'm so flustered, I can't figure out what 60 percent of $500,000 is," Mary said.

"It's about $300,000," Bill said, smiling.

"We could pay off the house," Mary said, amazed.

"Yes, we could," Thomas said, nodding.

"So," Bill said, "back to the conversation about getting into the mine."

"Right!" said Thomas.

"Right!" echoed Mary.

"I'll offer eight ounces of gold for thirty minutes of time in the mine," Bill said. "I might have to negotiate a little, so it could be more than eight ounces, but I think that's still the best way to do it. That way we don't have to sneak around, or pretend we might shoot somebody."

"I think we're in total agreement on that," Thomas said, looking at Mary to be sure he had that right. She nodded.

"All right," Bill said, "I'll let you know how that conversation goes. Could you put those bags back in the top drawer of my dresser?"

"Don't you think we should put this in the bank or something?" Mary asked.

"I guess we could get a safe deposit box," Bill said.

"I'll check on that tomorrow," Mary said. "Now that I know how much gold you're keeping in your sock drawer, I'm a little nervous about having it here."

Thomas nodded in agreement, and Bill said, "Yeah, now that you mention it, we should probably be keeping this at the bank."

Mary nodded, and said, "All right, it sounds like we're all in agreement. I'll make arrangements at the bank tomorrow while you talk to the mine owner."

"Agreed," said Thomas.

"Agreed," said Bill, reaching for the newspaper so he could finish reading it.

Chapter 16

November

"We need ball gowns," Caroline said. She was visiting with Mary, and they were talking about the Grand Promenade Ball that would be held on November 6th. It was a fundraising event that would raise money for the new Fourth Ward School that was planned. The Virginia Choral Society was going to start the event by singing a series of songs, and then the dance would begin at ten in the evening.

"You're right," Mary replied. "We do need ball gowns. Where's the best place to buy them?"

"You're just the funniest thing, sometimes," Caroline said. "We'll go to Mrs. Bishop's, of course. She'll make them for us."

"Oh, of course," Mary said. She had forgotten there weren't any pre-made ball gowns she could buy from a store. In 1869, most ball gowns were made by someone like Mrs. Bishop and her staff of seamstresses, sewing assistants, and trimmers. "When would you like to go to Mrs. Bishop's?" she asked.

"We should probably go soon. Do you have time this afternoon?" Caroline asked.

"Just let me grab a wrap and I'll be ready to go right now," Mary answered, heading to her bedroom for a shawl. "It's getting cold out there."

"Yes, it is, and I seem to have developed a bit of a cough," Caroline said. "My mother always said I had a weak chest. I guess she was right."

"Are you OK?" Mary asked. "Would you rather go to the dressmaker tomorrow?"

"Oh, heavens, no," Caroline laughed. "It's just a little cough. It'll clear up in no time. I'm fine."

They headed out the front door and walked down to C Street, strolling along the boardwalk until they came to number 67. A bell attached to the top of the door announced their arrival, and a woman with a long nose and steel-gray hair piled on top of her head joined them. She was very tall and thin, and had a measuring tape hanging around her neck. Mary noticed her fingers were bent and knobby, and she wondered if the dressmaker had arthritis.

Whether it was arthritis or something else, Mrs. Bishop's bent fingers didn't seem to slow her down. As soon as she heard that Mary and Caroline were there for ball gowns, she pulled several bolts of material from her shelves and spread out the various fabrics for the ladies to see.

"Oh, the dark green velvet is just beautiful," Mary said, and the woman nodded.

"Oh, yes, that color goes nicely with your eyes," she said. She unwrapped a longer portion from the bolt and expertly pinned a length of the fabric around Mary's shoulders. "Velvet has such a nice drape. This could be the perfect choice for you, don't you think?"

"Is it expensive?" Mary asked.

The woman looked at her with disapproval, and said, "Of course it is, my dear. But you didn't come here asking for a new apron. You came here for a ball gown."

"Oh," Mary said, a little taken aback. "I suppose you're right, but I will also need a dress for my twelve-year-old daughter. Do you have any fabric that is less, um, luxurious?"

"Yes," the woman said, unpinning the velvet fabric and rewinding it back onto the bolt. "For a twelve-year-old-girl I recommend a nice cotton fabric. Not for you, though."

She set the green velvet on the counter and selected two bolts of cotton fabric for Mary's inspection.

Mary smiled and said, "OK. The velvet for my dress, and the one with the bouquets of roses in the pattern for my daughter's dress. I'll send her to see you after school today, OK?"

"Yes, that will be fine," the dressmaker said, setting the rose bouquet-patterned bolt of cotton fabric on top of the green velvet. She walked to the doorway at the back of the store and called out, "Celeste! I'll need you to help with measurements."

Returning to the front of the store, she turned to Caroline. "And for you?" she asked.

"I'd like the burgundy satin," Caroline said. "With black lace accents, please."

"Oh, that will be stunning," Mary said.

Caroline smiled, and said, "I certainly hope so!"

On the day of the ball, Mary, Caroline, and Natalie spent most of the afternoon at the hairdresser. They sat for hours as several ladies pulled, braided, and knotted their hair, pinning it up at the top of their heads, and then extracting long strands that were curled around a hot iron. As each curl was completed, it was pulled down and interwoven with the last curl, creating a cascade that tumbled down the ladies' backs. It was a long and tedious process, but the results were spectacular. Natalie appreciated the look, but wondered how long it was going to take to undo the whole thing the next day.

That evening, after a generous dinner at Delmonico's Restaurant, the family split up and the ladies all went to Caroline's house to get dressed. The gentlemen, including Alex and Benjamin, would pick them up at 7:45 and escort them to the gala.

While the ladies were pulling the laces tight on each other's corsets, the men were pulling on black pants and stiffly starched white shirts with high collars. The ladies stepped into their hoop skirts next, and then put on their boots, while the men donned their dark gray vests, inserted cufflinks, and put on their shoes. As the ladies pulled their new ball gowns carefully over their freshly styled hair and secured the clasps on their necklaces, the men put on their black waistcoats, completing their outfits, too—except for the bow ties in their pockets. None of the men wanted to attempt the tricky business of tying a bowtie, so they all requested help with that final touch when they got to Caroline's house.

"We look fabulous!" Mary said, when everyone was finally ready to go. "I wish we could get a picture."

"I heard there will be a photographer at the Ball," Caroline said. "I don't know what he charges, but we could get a picture made while we're there."

Mary looked at Thomas, and he could tell how excited she was about the possibility.

"We will definitely try to get a picture," he said. "I have some money with me, and we'll ask about a photograph as soon as we get there, OK?"

Mary leaned over and kissed Thomas on the cheek. "Thank you, Sweetie," she said.

"Anything for you," he replied, gallantly, as he offered his arm. "Besides," he grinned, "you're right. We do look fabulous!"

As soon as they arrived at the school where the Ball was being held, they stopped in the lobby. A photographer was standing near the entrance, next to a draped camera positioned at the top of a tripod.

"Will you take our photograph?" Thomas asked.

"Yes, sir," the photographer replied. "The cost is two dollars."

"That's just fine," Thomas said. "Will you take the photo here in the lobby?"

"Yes, sir." the man said, "If you will just stand over there by the wall, I'll bring an extra chair over so all the ladies can be seated."

After a few minutes of politely adjusting some of their body positions and debating where the boys should stand, the photographer had everyone in place for the picture. He stood behind the camera and ducked his head under the drape. One arm held a small pan high above his head, and he counted, "One, two, three!" There was a quick flash in the pan, and then the man came out from under the drape.

"You can pick up your photograph after midnight," he told them, "or, if you prefer to pick it up on Monday, you are welcome to do so." He handed Thomas a card that read "Hedger & Noe Photographers. C & Taylor Streets, Virginia." On the back of the card, the man had written a number.

"Just present this card whenever you're ready to pick it up. The number on the back will identify your photograph."

"Thank you," Thomas said, putting the card in his pocket and paying the two-dollar fee. "We'll most likely be picking it up immediately after the ball."

"Very good, sir," the man said, crisply, as the group moved through the lobby to the school's auditorium, which had been decorated to serve as the dance hall.

They located seven chairs together and took their seats. People continued to trickle in during the choral performance, so that by the time the band started playing, the crowd had more than doubled. It was almost impossible to find an open spot on the dance floor, but the lack of space didn't seem to spoil anybody's good time. Alex set off in search of the table where Sarah and her parents were sitting, while Natalie and Benjamin went to find the table that had been reserved for their group. Everyone else made their way to the dance floor to join in the fun.

Caroline had given Alex a copy of *Beadle's Dime Ball-Room Companion and Guide to Dancing* several days ago, and he had practiced the correct way to ask a lady to dance.

"May I have the pleasure of dancing with you?" he asked when he arrived at Sarah's table.

Sarah looked up at him and smiled. "Thank you," she said, standing up from her chair. Alex offered his right arm to her, as *Beadle's Dime Ball-Room Companion* directed, and she slipped her hand around it. Before walking away from the table, Alex took an extra moment to nod to Sarah's parents.

"Sir," he said to her father.

"Ma'am," he said to her mother, and then he was guiding Sarah to the dance floor. She looked like a princess in her ball gown, and he felt very proud that she was going to be dancing with him.

There wasn't much room on the dance floor, so they squeezed in at one corner and kept their steps small. Eventually, they found themselves pushed along by the crowd, and not really dancing anymore. It was getting warm in the auditorium, and to Alex, the air felt stifling.

"Would you like to go outside for a few minutes to get some fresh air?" he asked.

They both looked at the table where her parents had been sitting, but their seats were empty. Sarah scanned the crowded dance floor but didn't see them anywhere.

"I would love to," she said, taking the chance that her parents were dancing and would never know she had behaved so boldly, "but I can't stay outside very long."

Alex said, "We'll just step out for a minute."

"All right," she said, and he opened the door.

Once they were outside, they both took several deep breaths. It was a relief to breathe in the cool night air.

"Thanks for coming out here with me," he said.

Sarah smiled, and said, "I'm glad you asked me. I enjoy spending time with you, even though I'm still trying to figure you out. You're different from the other boys I know."

"How am I different?" he asked.

"Oh, I suppose it's the way you ask me what I think about things. Most boys don't care what I think about. They aren't interested in my opinions. And then, there are the questions you ask. You seem to know so much about the world, but then you ask questions about the simplest things."

"What kind of questions?"

"Hmm," she thought for a moment, and said, "You ask questions like, 'what kind of music do you play in your house?' or 'what do you do during the summers?' or 'can't they do something about the smoke that comes out of the chimneys?' Things like that."

"I guess I like to understand things," Alex asked. "We've lived in different places, and I'm still getting used to Virginia City."

"I imagine it must be hard getting used to a new place," she said, looking up at him.

Alex looked into her eyes and felt his knees buckle a little. "Sometimes it is," he said, trying to sound casual. She was standing as close to him as she could, considering the hooped skirt of her ball gown. He was trying to decide what his next move should be, when she stood up on her tiptoes and kissed him.

216

Instinctively, he kissed her back. His heart was pounding so loudly in his chest that he was sure she must be able to hear it, and he briefly wondered if anybody ever died of a heart attack while they were kissing someone.

And then it was over. She stepped back down and looked away, suddenly shy. Alex's inner voice was shouting at him, "Kiss her again! Right now!" He hesitated for a second, but the voice urged him on. "Right now! Before it's too late!" And so, he did. *I should really listen to my inner voice more often,* he thought.

He might have stood there all night kissing Sarah, but she stepped away, and said, "My parents will be looking for me if I'm gone too long."

Alex came back to his senses and offered his arm. "Of course. We should go back inside."

She nodded and took his arm with both hands, possessing it in a way that felt different now. The dance hall was just as hot and stuffy as it had been five minutes earlier, but Alex didn't notice. He felt like he was floating as he walked Sarah back to her parents' table.

Meanwhile, Bill and Caroline had also escaped the crowded dance hall, exiting through a door on the other side of the auditorium. Holding hands, they strolled around the perimeter of the school several times, enjoying the night air. As they walked, they talked about how things hardly ever turn out the way you thought they would, and how much they enjoyed spending time with each other.

Suddenly, Bill could not imagine living the rest of his life without Caroline by his side, and he dropped to one knee.

"Caroline, I want to spend the rest of my life with you. I want to take care of you, and take long walks with you, and see your pretty face every morning. Will you marry me?"

Caroline gasped in surprise, covering her mouth with her hands. She stared at him for a moment, and then lowered her hands and smiled.

"Yes, Bill, I will marry you!" she said.

Bill smiled, too, and stood up, ignoring the cracking noises from his knees. He held her tight and kissed her, wanting to stay in the moment forever. Then he thought about how astonished the Taylors would be when they found out about his proposal. He had been impulsive and had just made things very complicated. He needed some time to figure things out before he talked to Thomas and Mary about it.

"I should have planned this better," he said to Caroline. "I would like to buy you a ring before we announce our engagement to anyone. Is that all right with you?"

"Of course," she said, trying not to sound disappointed about the delay. "When do you think that will be?"

"Tomorrow," Bill said. "Do you have time tomorrow to come with me and pick out a ring?"

Caroline took Bill's face in her hands and kissed him. "Oh, yes, Sweetheart," she said, "I have time."

"*You what?*" Thomas said, setting his cup of coffee back down on the table without taking a sip. Across the table, Mary sat, frozen. Her eyebrows were high on her forehead, and she was holding a fork full of scrambled eggs over her plate.

Bill had chosen this moment on purpose. Alex, Natalie, and Benjamin had already left for school, giving him an opportunity to talk to Thomas and Mary alone. The day before, Caroline had picked out a sapphire ring with small diamonds set around a center stone. The jeweler had measured her finger and told them the ring would be ready the next morning. As soon as Caroline finished her shift at the restaurant today, they were going to pick it up.

"I asked Caroline to marry me," Bill repeated.

Mary's eyes darted to the left, where her husband was sitting, and then back to Bill, sitting across the table. She slowly set her fork down on her plate. "But what are you going to do on December 26th?" she asked.

"I'm going to stay here," he said.

219

"You're not coming back with us?" asked Thomas.

"No," Bill answered, "I want to be with Caroline, and I think I can have a good life in this timeline."

"But what will we say when we go back, and people ask us where you are?" Mary asked.

"Nobody will ask you where I am," Bill answered. "Your family will walk out of the mine and go home. I doubt that anybody saw you go into the mine with me, and even if someone did, no one knows who you are or where you live. Nobody is going to pay any attention when you come out of the mine without me. I don't have any family that will worry about my disappearance. The owner of the mine is probably the only person who will be upset, and I'm going to write him a letter—which I will ask you to drop off at a Post Office in Reno before you leave."

"What about your friends?" asked Thomas.

"I'm going to write letters to them, too," Bill said. "I'll tell them I've decided to go to Australia and do some gold mining there for a while. I just need you to take those letters to Reno for me, and put them in the mail."

Mary and Thomas sat and looked at him. He gave them some time to process everything. After a couple of minutes, he broke the silence.

"It will work. Especially if you're willing to help me."

Mary's eyes started to fill with tears. "Are you sure this is what you want to do?" she asked.

"I'm sure," he answered, reaching across the table and taking her hand. "I've missed Becky every day since she died, and I will always love her, but somehow, Caroline has expanded my heart. I love her, too, and I want to stay with her."

After a minute, Mary wiped her eyes with her napkin. "OK," she said, putting the napkin back in her lap. "Can I help you plan the wedding?"

Smiling, Bill sat back in his chair. "I'm pretty sure Caroline would love that," he said.

Thomas pushed his chair away from the table and stood up. "It'll be hard to go back without you," he said, "But I'll do whatever you want. You're family, now."

Bill stood up, too, and took a step towards Thomas, holding out his hand. Thomas grabbed Bill's hand, and stepped around the corner of the table so he could pull his friend into a hug. He pounded Bill on the back with his free hand.

"You're gonna make me cry, man," he said.

"I know what you mean," Bill said, choking back his own tears and laughing at the same time.

Chapter 17

Thanksgiving

"Caroline reminded me today that Thanksgiving is just two weeks from now," Mary said. It was six o'clock in the evening, on the 11th of November. Thomas had come home thirty minutes earlier, after spending the day at the gold mining claims. It was getting dark much earlier in the evenings now, so he and Bill didn't stay out as late as they used to.

Mary was setting the table for dinner, working around the space where Thomas was sharpening their kitchen knives. Alex, Natalie and Benjamin were lying on the floor in front of the fireplace in the living room, playing a game of Snakes and Ladders, which was very similar to the Chutes and Ladders game they had played in their own time.

"For some reason, I thought I had more time. There's a lot of planning to do," she said, setting plates on the table in front of each chair. "I feel like I'm already behind schedule."

"What are you planning to serve?" Thomas asked.

"Caroline helped me with the menu. It's roast turkey, cranberry sauce, mixed pickles, coleslaw—or 'cold slaw,' as she calls it—mashed potatoes, tomatoes with boiled onions and corn, sweet potatoes, and roasted broccoli, and then mince, pumpkin, and apple pies for dessert."

"That sounds ambitious. Is she helping you with the cooking?"

"Oh, yes," Mary answered. "I probably wouldn't even attempt it without her. She's going to bring the cranberry sauce, sweet potatoes, 'cold slaw,' and the tomato, onion, and corn dish. We're going to roast the turkey and the broccoli here, and I'll make the mashed potatoes—Natalie can help with those. I'm also going to make the pies, but I can make those the day before. I think I can manage them on my own, as long as I can keep the oven temperature steady."

Just then, the front door opened, and Bill came in with a big smile on his face.

"It worked!" he said, as he shut the door behind him. "The superintendent of the Chollar-Potosi mine has agreed to suspend operations in the mine for thirty minutes on December 26th. We'll have access to it from 5:45 until 6:15 that evening, which will give everybody plenty of time to be in the right spot when the earthquake hits!"

"That's great!" Thomas exclaimed. "Did he accept eight ounces of gold as the payment?"

"Yep!" Bill said, taking off his hat and running his hand over his head. "I started out by offering him six ounces, and he asked for ten. So we settled on eight, which is exactly what we were hoping for. We'll give him the gold on December 25th, and count on him to uphold his end of the bargain. He has to plan the shutdown, so he wants the gold in advance. It's a little bit of a gamble, but he has a reputation for being an honest man. I've had a few drinks with him at the saloon, and he seems like a solid guy. A man's word goes a long way in this town. I trust him."

"All right," Mary said, "if you trust him, so do I."

"And that means we can stop worrying about how we'll be getting into the mine," Thomas said. "That's a relief."

"I agree!" said Bill, taking off his coat and hanging it on a peg near the front door. "It smells good in here. What's for dinner?"

"Pot roast with scalloped potatoes and green beans," Mary said proudly. "I made everything myself. And there's gravy, too!"

"That sounds wonderful," Bill said, "and I'm starved!"

"Well, you're just in time," Mary said. "Dinner is served!"

Two weeks later, Alex and Sarah sat together on a log at the far edge of the schoolyard, holding hands and watching, as the first snowflakes of the season drifted down. It was the day before Thanksgiving, and they knew they wouldn't see each other again until Monday.

"What is your family doing for Thanksgiving?" Sarah asked.

"We're just having a small family dinner, with my Uncle Bill and Caroline," Alex said. "How about you? What is your family doing?"

"The same. Just a small family gathering," she stuck out her tongue out to catch a snowflake.

"I can't believe it's almost December," Alex said. He had been thinking he should let Sarah know he wouldn't be coming back after Christmas, but he couldn't bring himself to say it. School would close for the winter break in five weeks, though, and he would have to tell her soon.

"I know what you mean," Sarah said. "My class will probably start making Christmas decorations as soon as we come back on Monday."

"I sincerely doubt that my class will be making Christmas decorations," Alex said. "I think my teacher is actually Ebenezer Scrooge wearing a Mr. White disguise."

Sarah broke into peals of laughter. "Wearing a Mr. White disguise," she said. "That's really funny."

"It would be even funnier if it wasn't true," Alex said, picking up a stick and tracing circles in the dirt with it. "He probably goes home at night and pulls the wings off flies to entertain himself."

Sarah threw him a sidelong glance. "You say the strangest things, sometimes," she said.

Alex kept tracing in the dirt with his stick. His life had become a jumbled mess of conflicting feelings, and he was struggling to handle them. On one hand, he was excited about going back to his own time, where he would see his friends and have television and videos and cell phones, and all the other conveniences he had been missing for almost five months. On the other hand, he really liked Sarah a lot—maybe he even loved her—and he was going to miss her. He was going to miss Uncle Bill and Caroline, too, and he wondered what it would feel like when he stepped back into his own time, knowing he would never see any of them again.

He sighed and threw the stick as far as he could. The snow was falling more heavily now, and the bell would ring soon, signaling the end of the lunch recess. Impulsively, he leaned over and gave Sarah a kiss. Startled, she pulled back a little, but then quickly kissed him back.

"You are going to get me in so much trouble!" she exclaimed, playfully pushing him away.

Alex smiled, and said, "I don't know what came over me. I couldn't help it. You look so beautiful with the snow falling around you."

She smiled back and him, and said, "Why, thank you, sir."

Across the schoolyard, they saw the front door of the school open. A teacher stepped out and looked around before she retreated into the building.

"We'd better head back. They'll be ringing the bell pretty soon." He had barely finished his sentence when the bell started to ring.

"See?" he said, standing up and holding out his hand to Sarah. She took his hand and stood up, and they walked across the schoolyard together. When they got to the steps he said, "I hope you have a nice Thanksgiving."

"You, too!" she said, lifting her skirt a little so she could run up the steps.

Alex stayed at the bottom of the steps and watched her disappear into the building. He turned around and watched the snow for a few seconds, and then he went up the steps, too.

It was still dark when Natalie woke the next morning. She lay there for a minute, wondering why she was awake, and then realized it was the noise from the kitchen that had awakened her. Her mother must be getting an early start on their Thanksgiving dinner. She stayed in bed for a few more minutes, enjoying the feeling of being warm under the covers, listening to the sounds of a meal being prepared.

Lately, she had been noticing—and appreciating—little things she hadn't ever paid attention to before the "time slip." As she drifted back to sleep she decided that listening to someone preparing a meal for you while you were warm and snug in your bed was a very cozy feeling.

Alex was listening to the sounds from the kitchen, too. After a few minutes, he gave up on the idea of going back to sleep and decided he was awake for the day. He threw back his covers and got out of bed, quietly slipping on his clothes. Picking up his shoes, he tiptoed out of the bedroom.

"Hi, Mom," he said, as he entered the kitchen. Mary was sitting at the table, peeling potatoes, and dropping them into a pot that was half-filled with water.

"Good morning!" she said. "I thought I'd get an early start on our dinner."

"I figured that's what you were doing. Do you need any help?"

"Oh, thank you for asking. Could you just bring in some wood for the stove?"

"Sure thing," Alex answered, heading for the front door. Pete was lying next to the stove, soaking up the warmth from the fire, but he looked up when Alex went past. When he saw Alex was heading toward the door, he jumped up and ran over to it, looking for an opportunity to go outside.

"All right, boy." Alex said, stepping out onto the porch, "come on. Let's get some wood."

Pete ignored the suggestion completely and did a running jump off the porch and into the street. He disappeared around the side of the house for a minute, and then came back, wagging his tail. Alex held out a small piece of wood from the stack he had in his arms, and Pete took it in his mouth. When they went back inside, Pete went to the wood basket by the stove and dropped the piece he was carrying into it. Alex followed and dumped his armload of wood into the basket, too.

"Thank you, gentlemen," his mother said, smiling. Pete shook himself off and then settled back down next to the stove.

Alex pulled out a chair across the table from his mother and spun it around so it faced the other way. "Do you ever think you're going to miss it here when we go back?" he asked, sitting down with his arms folded across the top of the chair back.

Mary looked up from the potato she was peeling and said, "Yes, I do. I feel like we've been talking to each other more since we've been here. Communicating better. We have more time for that, somehow."

"I know what you mean," Alex said. "I'm going to miss Uncle Bill and Caroline, too."

"I will, too," Mary said. "It's going to be very hard when we leave without them." After a minute, she went back to peeling potatoes, and said, "I'll bet you're going to miss some of the friends you've made here, too."

Alex grimaced. "Yeah. And they'll be gone-gone. I'll never see her again."

"You're talking about Sarah," Mary said. "That will definitely be a tough one."

Alex nodded. He didn't trust himself to speak.

"You know," Mary said, "there's a poem by Alfred Lord Tennyson that says, *tis better to have loved and lost, than never to have loved at all.*"

"I'm not so sure about that," Alex said, with his chin resting on his forearms.

"Well, I don't think he meant it's a good thing to have loved and lost, but I do think he's saying that you don't usually regret it when you let yourself love someone, even when you know it can't last. Everything ends, Sweetheart. It's about sharing those wonderful, beautiful moments with someone special for as long as you can. I think Tennyson is saying you should grab on to those moments with both hands, because, no matter how long they last, those moments... are going to be the highlights of your life."

Alex looked up at his mother and nodded. He waited for a few seconds to be sure he could trust his voice, and then said, "Thanks, Mom. You nailed that one."

Mary smiled just a little and went back to peeling potatoes. Alex stayed where he was for a few more minutes, watching her, and then said, "I think I'll take Pete for a walk and check out the sunrise."

Hearing his name, Pete lifted his head and wagged his tail a couple of times.

"Why don't you pick up a newspaper while you're out?" Mary suggested. "There's some change in the cup over there on the window ledge."

"Will do," Alex said. He looked at Pete and said, "Come on, boy. Do you want to go for a walk?"

With his nails scrambling for traction, Pete got up and ran over to the door. He stayed there, jumping up and down, until Alex opened it.

"I'll take that as a big yes," he said, watching Pete bolt through the open door.

Later that morning, Natalie and Benjamin dusted and swept the house while Mary scrubbed, sliced, chopped, and minced all the ingredients they would need that day. At ten, Bill went to Caroline's house to help her carry the food she had prepared, and Alex split the additional wood they would need for the stove and the fireplace.

Bill and Caroline arrived with their baskets of food at eleven o'clock. Even before they opened the door, they could hear loud banging noises coming from inside the house.

"Good Lord!" Bill said. "What are you banging on? We could hear it out in the street!"

"Ice," Thomas said, using the hammer in his hand to point to a large bowl full of cracked ice. "Mary is determined to have plenty of ice today. I got a ten-pound block. I'm almost done."

"Well, all right, then," Bill said, "hammer away."

He and Caroline set their baskets on the kitchen table, and Caroline immediately took an apron down from a hook in the kitchen.

"How can I help?" she asked, raising her voice to be heard over the racket.

"Will you just check the fire in the oven?" Mary shouted.

The banging noise stopped and Thomas said, "Finished!"

Mary continued in a normal voice, "The turkey should go in soon, and I want to be sure the temperature is right."

"Sure," Caroline said, opening the flour canister on the counter. She reached in and grabbed a pinch.

"I want to watch you do the flour," Natalie said to Caroline.

"Me, too," said Benjamin.

"All right," Caroline said, "come on over here, and you can watch it with me."

She opened the oven door and tossed the pinch of flour inside. All three of them watch the flour intently, as it slowly turned golden brown.

"It looks perfect," Caroline said to Mary, who was opening the jars of corn and stewed tomatoes. "Shall I put the turkey in now?"

"Yes, please," Mary said, reaching for a large mixing bowl.

Caroline lifted the pan with the turkey and then dropped it back down on the counter with a loud clang.

"Are you all right?" Mary asked, startled by the sudden noise.

"I don't know what came over me," Caroline said. "All of a sudden that turkey felt like it weighed a hundred pounds."

"Well, just leave it there, and I'll take care of it in a minute," Mary said. "Do you need to sit down?"

"Oh, well, um," Caroline said, vaguely. She looked around, as though she was trying to find something, and then she pulled out a chair from the table. "I believe I will sit, for just a minute."

Mary left her opened jars on the counter and hurried over to her friend. "Are you all right?" she asked again.

Caroline could see the concern on Mary's face, and tried to reassure her. "I think it was the walk over here with the food basket that did me in," she said, smiling a little. "I'll be fine in just a minute."

Bill came into the kitchen to see what was happening. "I knew I should have carried both baskets," he said, looking worried. "Are you all right, Sweetheart?"

Caroline waved her hand in front of her face. "Oh, please, I'm fine. I just need to catch my breath."

"Well, I think I'll just sit right here next to you," Bill said, reaching for a chair.

"You will not!" Caroline said. "Oh, my goodness, no. You need to take yourself right out of this kitchen. You can't be underfoot while we're trying to cook." She stood up and smiled at him. "See? All better. Now scoot!"

"Yes, ma'am," Bill said, smiling, as he pushed his chair back under the table.

"Let me get the turkey and put it in the oven," Mary said. "How about if you finish opening those jars over there?"

"Sure thing," Caroline said, heading over to the counter. "Whatever you need."

The rest of the meal preparation went smoothly, and the family sat down to a feast at 3:30 that afternoon. They discussed Caroline's wedding plans while they ate, and Mary realized she would have to adjust her thinking to match the wedding Caroline had in mind.

"Really?" Mary asked. "You just want your friends from the restaurant and our family there? What about your family?"

"I don't have any family to invite," Caroline said, without a hint of self-pity. "I was an only child, and my father died when I was very young. I never married, and when my mother died, I came here to Virginia City to see if I could make my fortune." She smiled, and said, "I figured out pretty quickly that everybody has to eat, whether they find gold or silver, or nothing at all, so I used most of my inheritance to buy a twenty-five percent share of the restaurant."

They all looked at her in astonishment. "You own twenty-five percent of the restaurant?" Bill asked. "I thought you just worked there."

Caroline shrugged, and said, "Surprise! It was a pretty safe bet. Everybody really does have to eat."

"That was brilliant!" Mary said with admiration. "I had no idea you were a businesswoman."

"That's how I can afford to buy ball gowns," Caroline said with a smile.

The conversation continued through the rest of their meal, and then into the living room when they were finished. After a while, Bill suggested they "divide and conquer" the kitchen.

"And what would that entail?" Mary asked.

"How about if the guys wash all the pots and pans, and then you ladies wash all the dishes, glasses, and silverware?" he suggested.

"That sounds like a great idea to me!" Caroline said.

"I like it, too," Mary said, settling back into her chair.

"Works for me," Natalie added, opening up a deck of cards to play a few rounds of Solitaire.

When the men finished scrubbing the pots and pans, they swapped locations, and the women headed into the kitchen to fulfill their part of the bargain.

"Do you want to come sit on the porch for a while, Uncle Bill?" Alex asked.

Bill and Thomas exchanged a look. It was cold outside, and the front porch was not as inviting as it had been during warmer weather.

"Sure," Bill said, assuming that Alex must have something on his mind he didn't want to discuss in front of everybody else. The two of them put their coats on and headed outside. Pete, as always, took advantage of the open door and joined them.

"What's on your mind?" Bill asked after Alex shut the door behind them.

Taking a seat on one of the porch chairs, Alex said, "It's Sarah."

"OK," said Bill, pulling up a chair for himself. "What about Sarah?"

"I really like her a lot. I actually think I love her," Alex said, "and I have to leave her when we go back home."

"Yes, that's true," Bill said, waiting to see what else Alex had to say.

"Will you watch out for her after I leave?" Alex asked. "Her parents are pretty wealthy, and I'm sure they'll take care of her, but if you ever find out that she needs something, will you please try to help her?"

"Yes, of course," Bill said, realizing how important this was to Alex. "I'll watch out for her for as long as I am able."

"Thank you," Alex said, holding out his hand for a handshake. "I appreciate it."

Bill reached over and shook Alex's hand firmly. "You're a good person. I'm proud to be your Uncle Bill."

Alex sat quietly in his seat for another minute and then went back into the house. Bill hung back on the porch and quickly wiped his eyes with his handkerchief. He was going to miss this family very much when they left.

Chapter 18

For Better or Worse

"Let me help you with that," Mary said, as Caroline struggled with the bodice lacing at the front of her wedding dress.

"It just doesn't want to fit right. I think I have the laces pulled as tight as they'll go."

"You picked this dress up a couple weeks ago, right?" Mary asked.

"Yes, and it seemed to fit so much better when I first got it. Maybe I don't have it laced up right."

Mary checked the laces, but they looked fine to her. She tried pulling them tighter. "That helped a little," she said, "but I think we need to take the sides in a bit more. It'll only take a minute or two."

"Oh, all right," Caroline sighed. "I think you're right."

She stepped back out of the dress and handed it to Mary, who was already pulling white thread through a needle for the quick alteration. She sat down on her bed and waited while Mary ran the needle through the fabric on either side of the bodice.

"How much time do we have?" she asked.

"We're supposed to be at the church in twenty minutes," Mary said with her head bent over her work, "but even if we're late, they won't start without you."

Caroline laughed, and said, "I guess they won't." She coughed and then took a breath. "I'm so tired of this darned cough. I'll be very glad when it goes away."

"Finished!" Mary said. "And in record time. Let's see how it fits now."

Caroline stepped back into the dress and pulled the laces together one more time. "That's so much better!" she said. "Thank you."

"I'm glad I could help," Mary said. "Now, let's get you over to the church!"

They hurried out the front door, and Mary stopped to lock it. She lingered there, facing the door for a few seconds, biting her lip. Caroline had lost a lot of weight in a very short amount of time and she had been fighting that cough for weeks. Mary was worried that her friend might be a lot sicker than she realized.

"But this is not a day for worrying," she whispered to herself. She turned and hurried down the steps.

"This is going to be the best day ever!" she said to Caroline, when she caught up to her in the front yard.

They climbed into the carriage that was waiting for them and settled in for the brief ride to the church.

"Are you nervous?" Mary asked.

"I'm excited," Caroline said. "And maybe a little nervous, too."

"Well, you look beautiful, and Bill is a good man," Mary assured her.

"I don't have any doubt about that," Caroline said, smiling.

They finished the ride in silence, arriving at the church a few minutes later. Mary got out of the carriage first.

"Wait here for just a minute while I check to see where Bill is," she said. "He shouldn't see you until you're walking down the aisle."

Caroline waited in the carriage until Mary came back.

"Everyone is in place, and the pianist has started playing. We can go in now. Are you ready?"

"I am very ready," Caroline answered. "Let's not keep everybody waiting any longer."

Holding Mary's hand for support, Caroline stepped down from the carriage. Mary escorted her friend from the carriage to the foyer of the church, where Thomas was waiting for them, holding a bouquet of pink roses with white baby's breath flowers. He handed the bouquet to Caroline and kissed her on the cheek, and then offered his arm to Mary.

Thomas and Mary walked up the aisle to join Bill, who was waiting at the altar. Mary stood on the left side, waiting for Caroline, while Thomas joined Bill on the right.

The minister came to the podium and the piano music got louder. The guests stood up and turned to watch as Caroline walked up the aisle to join Bill at the altar. When she reached him, they turned to face each other, and the congregation took their seats. Bill lifted Caroline's veil and carefully placed it behind her head. Then he took both of her hands in his.

"Dearly beloved," the minister said, beginning the wedding vows.

Three weeks later, Caroline looked out the front window of the house she and Bill were now sharing, and said, "There's a carriage parked out front."

"I know," Bill said, "I made arrangements yesterday so we could ride in style to the doctor's office, instead of walking."

"It's not that far," she protested, "I can walk."

"Let me spoil you a little," Bill said. "At least this one time."

Caroline put on her cloak and pulled the hood up over her head.

"All right," she said, "but this is ridiculous."

Bill reached over and took her hand. It felt small and fragile, and he was worried about how sick she had been for the last few days. He was glad she had agreed to see the doctor.

"Your carriage awaits, my lady," he said, gallantly, holding her hand to steady her on the steps down to the street. When they got to the carriage, he stepped behind her and put his hands around her waist to lift her up into the carriage. She was lighter than he expected, and she gasped in surprise as she rose quickly to her seat.

"You might give me a little warning next time."

"I'm sorry," Bill said, trying to ignore the fear in his gut about how much weight she had lost. "You're right. I didn't mean to startle you."

The doctor's office was just a down the street, so it only took a few minutes to get there. Bill helped Caroline down from the buggy and then escorted her into the waiting area.

"Is the carriage just going to wait there?" Caroline asked, holding the curtain to one side and peering through the front window of the doctor's office.

"Yep. He'll give us a ride back to the house when we're finished here."

"That really is a waste of money, Sweetheart," Caroline said, picking up Bill's hat from the chair next to him and holding it in her lap when she sat down.

"It's not a waste when it gives me a chance to treat you like a queen," Bill said, smiling at her and doing his best to look unconcerned.

A moment later, the doctor came into the waiting room and asked, "Mrs. Johnson?"

Caroline reached for Bill's arm and they both stood up. He took his hat from her and held it at his side while she held onto him, steadying herself.

"Right this way," said the doctor, motioning for them to enter the examination room. He followed behind them and pulled the door shut.

Twenty minutes later, the door opened again, and Caroline stepped back into the waiting room, dabbing her eyes with her handkerchief. Bill followed behind her. His face looked like it was set in stone.

"I'm sorry we can't do more," the doctor said, "but Consumption is a fairly slow disease. Sometimes, people live for two or three years. Some people live even longer than that. You'll have some time to put your affairs in order."

"Thank you, doctor," Bill said, gruffly, putting on his hat. He gently tucked Caroline's hand into the crook of his arm and led her to the carriage that was waiting for them.

Neither one of them spoke during the ride back to their house.

As soon as they got back to the house, Caroline went into the living room and sat on the couch, out of breath from walking up the stairs to their front door. She stared into space. Bill sat down next to her and took her hand. He sat with her for a few minutes, just holding her hand. Then he said, "I have something to tell you."

She looked at him with red-rimmed eyes, but didn't say anything.

He cleared his throat, and said, "I know what the doctor said about Consumption, and I know you think it's fatal, but I know better. I know there is a cure."

"No, there really isn't," Caroline said, not looking at him.

"Yes, there is," Bill insisted. He paused, and then said, "It just hasn't been invented yet."

"That may be true," Caroline said, turning to look at him, "but unless somebody invents a cure really soon, it will be too late to do me any good."

"You're right," Bill said. "It's going to take quite a while. If I remember right, it will be at least fifty years before there's a cure. Maybe more."

"Pardon me?" asked Caroline, confused about what he was saying.

Bill shifted on the sofa so he was facing her. "Please keep an open mind, and let me finish talking before you say anything, OK?"

She looked at him for a long moment and then said, "OK."

Reaching over, he took her other hand in his, holding both of them now, as though he wanted to be sure she wouldn't bolt away while he was talking.

"Sweetheart, the Taylor family and I came here from the future, about a hundred and fifty years from now. We accidentally slipped into this time during an earthquake. We were all planning to go back to our own time during the next earthquake, but then I met you and decided to stay here. But now I think you and I should both go back to my time, where there is a cure for Consumption and we can be happy and live together for a long time." He stopped talking, watching to see how she would react.

She sat perfectly still for a couple of minutes without speaking. *Bill must have lost his mind.* Her diagnosis must have been too much for him. She had seen enough heartbreak on the Comstock to know it could happen. His talk about time travel couldn't be true, and she was sad that she was the cause of his mental breakdown.

"This is a lot to think about," she said, gently.

"Yes, I know it is," Bill said, aware that he hadn't convinced her, yet. "Mary and Thomas will tell you it's true, and they'll understand why I told you about this when they find out how sick you are. I'll go with you, and you can ask them."

Caroline thought about the Taylors for a moment. There were so many simple, day-to-day things Thomas and Mary didn't seem to know. The Taylor children were odd, too. Sweet, but odd. Then she remembered the strange commentary from the whole family while during the base ball games. Still, none of these things were enough to convince her they had come from the future. She kept searching her memory for something—anything—that would let her believe what Bill was saying.

While Bill waited for Caroline to say something, he wracked his brain, trying to think of anything else he could do or say that would be convincing. Suddenly, he had an idea.

"Wait here," he said, standing up from the couch. "I'll be right back."

He hurried out of the room and went upstairs to their bedroom, taking two steps at a time to get there faster. Opening the closet door, he dropped to his knees and reached to the back corner, where he kept a small box of quartz crystals he had collected while he was mining for gold. He dumped the box out onto the floor and grabbed the coin he had hidden beneath the crystals. Clutching it in his hand, he hurried back down the steps.

"I have something to show you," he said, as came back into the living room. "But first I want to tell you a little more about my first wife, Becky."

Caroline looked at him with a puzzled expression and said, "OK."

"Becky was born in Wyoming. The state of Wyoming, not the territory that it is today. It became a state in 1890."

He couldn't read her face, so he opened his hand to show her the coin he had retrieved from the back of the closet, and continued.

"This is a United States quarter that was minted in the year 2007. It commemorates the state of Wyoming."

He stretched his arm out, offering the quarter to her. She hesitated for a moment and then took it from him.

"Do you see where it says 'The Equality State' on the front?" he asked.

Caroline looked at the coin and nodded.

"That's because they were the first state in the union to grant women the right to vote. The state motto is 'Equal Rights.' Becky was very proud of that." He paused for a moment, and took a breath.

"I used to carry this coin with me all the time. It made me feel closer to Becky, but I've had to keep it hidden since we've been here, in 1869."

He waited anxiously while Caroline examined the quarter, turning it over and over.

"We buried the rest of the money from our time in the backyard right after we moved in to the house," he told her, hoping she was starting to believe him.

She looked up at him and said, "I know you loved Becky very much."

"Yes," he said. "And I love you very much, too. We can go over to the house and dig up the rest of the money, if you want."

Caroline put the quarter back in Bill's hand. He closed his fingers around it and searched her eyes. She held his gaze for a moment. Then she asked, "So, how does it work? How does a person ride an earthquake into another time?"

"So, you believe me?" Bill asked.

"I want to believe you," she said, "but this is hard to comprehend and I have a lot of questions."

"I'll answer your first question right now," he said. "You don't actually ride an earthquake. It's more like the earthquake opens a door. The door opens and you walk through. It's pretty simple. You just have to be in the right place when it opens."

"And where is the right place?"

"The Chollar Mine. To be more accurate, in today's time it's called the Chollar-Potosi Mine because there was a merger."

Caroline nodded and said, "I know what it's called."

"Right," Bill said, "Let me try again. The door to my time is in the Chollar-Potosi Mine, and it is going to open on December 26th, at 6:00 in the evening."

"And you know this—how?" Caroline asked. "Can you predict earthquakes in the future?"

"No, we can't predict earthquakes, but the one that's coming on December 26th is part of the history of Virginia City, and I'm certain we'll be able to travel back to my time during the earthquake because I've done it once before."

He watched to see how she would react to that news.

Caroline clasped her hands together in her lap. "So you're saying that you've been in 1869 before, and you traveled back to your time through a door in the Chollar-Potosi mine?"

"Yes!" he exhaled loudly. He hadn't realized he was holding his breath. "That's what happened. Almost. It isn't exactly a door, though, it's more like an opening. And the first time I stepped through it I ended up in 1868. Then I went back to my time about an hour later."

"And how long have you been in 1869?" she asked. She shook her head a little at the strangeness of the question.

"Since the Fourth of July," he told her. "In my time, I am a tour guide for the Chollar Mine, and I was giving the Taylor family a tour when we had an earthquake. The earthquake opened the portal—the doorway—to 1869, and we accidentally went through it."

Caroline listened carefully as Bill continued his explanation.

"The first time it happened, I didn't know what to do, so I stayed right there at the mine and pretended to be a miner. I heard people talking about things they had planned for the next year, which is how I figured out it was 1868. I was only here for an hour, though, and then a second earthquake hit. I went back through the opening during that second earthquake. It took me back to the exact time that I left—or pretty close to it."

Bill stopped talking and waited for Caroline's reaction.

After a minute she asked, "So you believe I can walk through this doorway—this opening—with you and the Taylors on December 26th, and we'll all be in the future?"

"Yes. Absolutely."

Caroline nodded. "What is it like in the future?" she asked.

Bill thought quickly about the best way to answer that question. He didn't want to overwhelm her with too much information, so he decided to start with small things.

"Well, we have machines that wash the dishes," he said with a little smile.

"Really?" she asked. "That sounds very nice."

"Yes, and we have carriages that don't need to be pulled by horses."

"What about washing clothes? Is there a machine that does that?" she asked.

"Oh, yes, there are washing machines and drying machines for clothes," he said.

"So, what do people do? It sounds like they sit around all day while machines do everything for them."

"Well, there *are* a lot of machines that do things for us, but that gives people more time to do the things they want to do."

"And you're saying there's a cure for Consumption in your time?" she asked.

"Yes, there is," Bill said, "but it's not called Consumption. It's called Tuberculosis."

"Tuberculosis," she said. "Why did they change the name?"

"I don't know," Bill answered, "but we can find out when we get there."

"Could we come back to 1869 after I'm cured?"

"I don't think so. Both times I've traveled to the past were an accident. I don't know how to open the doorway on purpose."

Caroline nodded.

"But you would be alive," Bill said earnestly, "and you wouldn't be sick, and we would be together. I will always protect you and love you, no matter where we are. Or when we are."

Caroline took his hand and kissed the back of it.

"You were going to change your whole life for me, and I had no idea," she said. "I'm so lucky to have found you, and I'm lucky you love me as much as you do. I love you, too! I want a long life with you, and I know for sure that won't be possible if I stay here."

"So you believe me? You'll go with me?"

"Yes. I'll go with you. I'll go wherever you're going on December 26th."

"Yes!" Bill jumped up from the couch and pulled her to her feet. Her thoughts were in a whirl, but she smiled at him as he wrapped his arms around her.

"You're safe with me," he said, holding her tight. "I promise."

Chapter 19

Cold Winter Days

Caroline handed her keys to the restaurant's new partner.

"It's a good business," she said. "If you treat people right, they'll keep coming back." Then she smiled, and added, "If you don't treat people right, I will come right back here and make your life miserable!"

She turned and walked to the front door, placing her palm on the doorframe for a moment before continuing out to the street. She was leaving the Star Restaurant for the last time, and she was sad that this chapter of her life was ending.

Bill was waiting for her outside, and she took his arm.

"Are you all right?" he asked.

She nodded, and said, "I will be."

They walked home slowly, arm in arm. It was December 22nd, and they had just a few days left before *The Big Day*, as Mary called it. Caroline paid special attention to her surroundings as they walked, knowing the town would be different in the future. Bill had explained to her they were doing their best, in his time, to preserve the history of Virginia City, but she knew it wouldn't be the same as the Virginia City she could see today.

Turning to Bill, she said, "I'm going to remember this Christmas forever. I want to finish decorating the house and cook a big goose with all the fixings. I want to create a memory that will be as perfect as it can be."

"Just tell me what I can do to help you make that happen," Bill said.

"You don't need to worry about that," she laughed. "I'll definitely tell you what you can do to help."

She was quiet for a minute, and then said, "Starting tomorrow, I'm going to do everything I can to make the next chapter of our lives together as happy as they can be. But, you know, I'm going to give myself this one afternoon to be sad about leaving."

Bill reached his arm around her shoulders and pulled her a little closer. He matched his stride to hers, and they walked the rest of the way home together, snuggled close.

Some distance away, Alex was also taking this moment to be sad about the end of this chapter in his life. He and Sarah were sitting in their usual spot across the schoolyard, and he knew it was the last time he would see her. He felt like a coward for having waited so long to tell her.

"Sarah," he said, holding her hand tight. "I have to tell you something, and I really wish I didn't."

"What is it?" she asked, looking worried.

"My family is moving away from Virginia City during the winter break. We won't be coming back."

Sarah looked at the ground. After a moment, a tear slid down her cheek, and Alex felt a lump rising in his throat. Now that Uncle Bill and Aunt Caroline were going back with them, he couldn't even assure her they would watch out for her after he left.

"I'm so sorry," he said. "I hate this."

"We could write to each other," she said, looking up at him. "And maybe you could come back."

Alex struggled to find the right words. He wanted to tell her everything, to explain why he wouldn't be able to write to her or come back to see her. It wasn't fair that he couldn't tell her the truth.

"I wish I didn't have to go," he said, surprised to hear himself say it out loud. Until this moment, it hadn't occurred to him that he could choose to stay.

"I wish that, too," Sarah said, looking back down at the ground.

Alex thought about what it would be like if he did stay, but just a few seconds later he knew he couldn't make a huge decision like that without having more time to think it through and plan for it. His family would be devastated if he didn't go back with them, and no matter how he felt about Sarah, he knew he wasn't prepared to be on his own in her timeline.

He decided to tell her something that was true, even if it wasn't the whole truth. "I have to go with my family," he said, "but I'll do my best to come back." *All I have to do is figure out how to open the portal*, he thought to himself.

"Where are you going?" she asked. This time, he told her a lie. "New York," he said, deciding it would be best if she thought he was far away. "But, I'll do my best to come back when I can." Then, for the first time, he told her, "I love you."

Another tear rolled down Sarah's cheek, and they leaned towards each other to share a kiss. Then she brushed her tears away and said, "I love you, too. No matter what happens, I will always love you. Nothing will ever change that."

She reached up and untied the ribbon in her hair. Then she reached for Alex's hand and laid the ribbon across his palm. She curled his fingers around it and said, "I'll wait for you—for as long as I can."

She kissed him one more time, and then she stood up. Alex stood up, too, watching as she turned and ran across the schoolyard, her long hair flying out behind her. He wanted to memorize everything about this moment.

When she disappeared through the front doors of the school, his eyes filled with tears and his vision blurred. She couldn't hear him, but he said it anyway—"I'll always love you, too."

The school bell signaled the end of the lunch recess, but he ignored it. He sat down on the log and watched as the other students went into the building. Then he saw Natalie and Benjamin across the schoolyard, walking towards him.

"I think we're done with school here," Natalie said when they reached the spot where Alex was sitting.

Alex stood up and put Sarah's ribbon in his pocket. He wiped his eyes, and said, "I think so, too."

Benjamin reached out and took Alex's hand in his, and for the last time, the three of them walked home from school in Virginia City.

Chapter 20

Christmas... And The Big Day

"Merry Christmas!" Bill and Caroline said together as they opened the door.

"Merry Christmas!" said each of the Taylors as they entered the house, following the couple into the living room.

"I love the wreath you have on the front door," Mary said. "Did you make that yourself?"

"I wish I could say yes, but, no, I bought it in town," Caroline said. "I like the intense colors of the red berries and the dark green holly leaves."

"I do, too," Mary said. "It's very Christmas-y."

"The goose will be ready in about ten minutes," Caroline said. "Bill was a big help. He gets credit for the stuffing. He says it's an old family recipe."

"Where is your Christmas tree?" Benjamin asked, as he looked around.

"It's right over here, in the corner," Caroline said, pointing to a small tree in a pot that was sitting on an end table.

"It's very small," Benjamin said, "and you don't have any lights."

"Benjamin! That's a rude thing to say to Aunt Caroline," Mary scolded. "Christmas trees are different here than they are at home. Do you see the decorations on the tree? Every one of those decorations was made by hand. That makes them special."

"I'm sorry, Aunt Caroline," Benjamin said, "I didn't mean to be rude, and I like your special decorations."

Caroline smiled at him and said, "That's OK, Ben, I know this is a little different than what you're used to."

She looked up at Thomas and Mary and said, "It feels strange and sad not to be giving gifts to each other, don't you think?"

Mary nodded, and Thomas said, "It *is* a little sad, but what would we do with them?"

"We'll have another opportunity for a Christmas gift exchange in six months or so," Mary said. "Kind of a 'do-over' I suppose."

Caroline smiled and excused herself to go check on the goose. Mary started to follow her into the kitchen, but Bill stopped her.

"I think she wants a minute to herself," he said. "She knows I just checked the goose."

"I can't imagine how she must be feeling," Mary said. "We're all excited to be going home, but she's leaving everything she knows and loves behind— except for you, of course, Bill."

"Well, she knows and loves you guys, too," Bill said. "It will take a little time, but there isn't much of a future for her here, and I keep reminding her she's going to feel so much better after she gets some twenty-first century medical treatment. On the days she's not feeling well, she can't wait for December 26th to get here."

"Still," Thomas said, "it has to be hard for her. We'll all do our best to be sensitive to her feelings. Right, guys?"

Mary, Alex, Natalie, and Benjamin all nodded their heads.

"Well, have a seat, everybody," Bill said, gesturing to the couch and chairs in the living room. "We have a few minutes to relax."

As they took their seats, Mary said, "While we're waiting for dinner, I would really like to hear what everybody's favorite memory will be when we go back to our own time."

"That's easy," Natalie said. "My favorite memory is hanging out at the C & C pond with Teddy."

"My favorite memory is the Grand Promenade Ball," Mary said.

"What a coincidence," Caroline said, as she came back from the kitchen, "the Grand Promenade Ball is one of my favorite memories, too!" She smiled and winked at Bill.

"Well, I don't know if it's a favorite memory," Bill said, "but I will never forget the looks on your faces when I told you I had asked Caroline to marry me!"

Everyone had a good laugh about that, and then Benjamin offered his favorite memory.

"The circus! That was my favorite," he said.

"But you got lost," Alex said.

"No, I didn't," Benjamin said. "I knew where I was the whole time."

"Well, he's got a point there," Bill said, and everybody laughed again.

"I think my favorite memory was being the best man at your wedding," Thomas said. "That was pretty special."

He cleared his throat and ducked his head, studying his fingernails for a minute.

"Thank you for that, buddy," Bill said, acknowledging the moment.

Alex said, "I don't really want to talk about my favorite memory, but the day I found that big gold nugget was a pretty good day."

Since everyone knew Alex's favorite memory was probably about Sarah, they all nodded.

"That *was* a doozy!" Bill said, as Caroline got up from her seat to give Alex a hug.

"How about if we all go to the kitchen?" she asked. "Each person can grab a dish and take it with them to the table. I'll bring the lemonade and a bottle of wine."

In just a few minutes, the food was on the table and everyone was seated at the dining room table, except for Bill. A minute later, he came into the dining room, carrying the Christmas goose on a silver platter. He set it down carefully and everyone clapped with appreciation. Bill remained standing, and after a few seconds, he tapped his glass with a spoon.

"I'm not much good at things like this, but I think you all know what's in my heart. It has been a privilege to be a part of this family, and I want each of you to know how much I care about you."

"Hear, hear," Thomas said, raising his wine glass. Everyone else raised their glasses, too, and Thomas said, "I believe I can speak for all of us when I say the feeling is mutual. Here's to the Taylor-Johnson family!"

Glasses were clinked all around, and then Bill started carving the Christmas goose. Caroline encouraged everyone to help themselves to the dish that was closest to their plate, and then pass it on around the table.

By the end of the evening, they had all eaten as much as they could, and then topped that off with a piece of mincemeat pie. When they were finished, they moved to the living room to relax with some cinnamon-flavored coffee or tea.

"Hey, look! It's snowing outside!" Benjamin said.

They all gathered at the living room windows and watched the snow falling down to the ground in big flakes. Against the darkened sky, and illuminated by the gas lamps that lined Virginia City's streets, it looked like gold was floating down to cover the city.

"It's magic," Mary said, pulling her family close. "Yes, indeed," Bill said, holding Caroline snugly in his arms. "It is definitely magic."

The next evening there was a quick knock at the front door of the Taylor's house, and then Bill and Caroline stepped inside.

"Is everybody ready?" Bill asked.

"I think so," Mary answered from across the living room. "I just finished the mopping the kitchen floor."

Bill smiled and said, "Your landlord has no idea what a great tenant you are. I really doubt that anybody else would mop the floor."

"It feels important that we leave everything in good shape," Mary said. She took off her apron and reached around the corner to hang it up on the hook in the kitchen. "What time is it?"

"It's 5:00," he said. "We should start walking over to the mine pretty soon."

"All right, guys," Mary called out to her family, "it's time to go." She picked up the picture they had taken at the Grand Promenade Ball and the journals she had purchased for Alex and Natalie, and tucked them into a clean flour sack. She turned to Bill and said, "You know we're bringing Pete, right?"

"I'm not surprised," he answered. "I don't see how you could leave him behind."

Alex, Natalie, Benjamin, and Thomas emerged from their bedrooms, ready to go. Inside Natalie's right shoe were the two nickels that Teddy Roosevelt had given her.

"We're ready," Alex said, triple-checking his pocket to be sure he had Sarah's ribbon.

"I feel silly asking," Bill said to Thomas, "but do you have all of your gold?"

"It's right here," Thomas said, smiling, as he patted the pockets of his pants and his jacket. "It weighs a lot! I had to tighten my belt to keep my pants from sliding down!"

Bill laughed and said, "All right then, shall we go?"

"We shall," Thomas said, opening the front door.

"Come on, Pete!" Benjamin called. "Follow us!"

Mary closed the door behind them and locked it. She put the key under the doormat and said, "Surely the landlord will check there, don't you think?"

"I'm sure he will," Thomas said, taking her hand and leading her down the steps and into the street.

They arrived at the Chollar-Potosi mine at 5:30. Bill went to the Superintendent's Office to check in and came back to the group a minute later.

"He said we can go in at 5:45 on the dot. There are still a couple of miners who haven't left yet, and he doesn't want us bumping into each other."

They stood there waiting for time to pass, each one lost in their own thoughts. Finally, the Superintendent stepped out of his office and said, "OK, folks, she's all yours."

"This is it," Caroline said. "This is really it."

Bill put his arm around her shoulders and said, "Yes, and I'll be with you every step of the way."

They all headed into the mine, and Bill led them to the spot where he knew the silver would be showing through in the future.

"This is the place," he said. "We'll just wait right here."

They stood there, expectantly, for a few minutes, and then Mary started lifting her feet up and down.

"Oh! Oh!" she exclaimed.

"What is it?" Thomas asked, alarmed.

She pointed straight down. Their eyes were still adjusting to the dim candlelight in the mine, so it took a few seconds before they could see what she was pointing at. On the floor, a big furry blanket was moving quickly towards the entrance of the mine. A big furry blanket that was made of...

"Rats!" Alex said. "I forgot about them!"

"Just stand still and let them run past us," Bill said. "They're not interested in us. They can sense the earthquake that's coming."

"Oh, dear," said Caroline.

Pete began barking furiously, adding to the commotion. Benjamin held tightly to the the rope tied to Pete's collar, and wrapped an extra length around his wrist.

"Well, this is not how I imagined it would be. I completely forgot about the rats," Thomas said.

At that moment, Pete lunged forward, trying to catch one of the rats. The rope slipped from Benjamin's hand and unwrapped itself from his wrist. In a flash, Pete was gone.

"Ow!" Benjamin cried out, rubbing his wrist where the rope had burned it. Then, despite the pain in his wrist, he bolted towards the mine entrance, trying to catch Pete before he got too far away.

"Benjamin! No!" Mary yelled "Come back here!"

Brushing past her, Alex joined the chase, trying to catch his little brother. A few seconds ticked by while they all stared at the entrance to the mine, trying to decide what to do.

"I've got them!" Alex called out, from somewhere nearby, "I've got them, both!"

"Hurry!" Bill yelled, checking his pocket watch. The second hand seemed to be moving in slow motion. It landed thunderously on each mark, and Bill watched as three more seconds ticked by before both boys and the dog appeared at the entrance to the mine.

Benjamin picked Pete up, and held him against his chest. Alex grabbed his brother's free hand and pulled him into the mine, shouting, "Come on! Run!"

The ground was shifting beneath them, but Benjamin ran as fast as he could, holding his dog tightly. Another wave rippled through the mine, and both boys struggled to stay on their feet. They staggered forward as the rest of the family watched anxiously.

"Come on!" Natalie yelled to them.

"Hurry!" Thomas shouted, taking a step in their direction. He held his hand out as far as he could, straining to reach his sons. He could see that a patch of silver was becoming visible on the wall next to him.

Alex took one more lunging step and grabbed his father's hand. As the ground shifted beneath their feet, both father and son tightened their grip.

Alex focused all of his energy on holding tightly to his brother and father. He felt himself being pulled in both directions.

The constant background noise of 1869 Virginia City began to fade away…

until finally…

there was silence.

EPILOGUE

Present day

The Johnsons and the Taylors made it safely back to their own time, two hours and fifty-four minutes after they had first stepped through the Chollar Mine portal. Alex did the math and calculated that one minute had passed in their time for each day they had spent in 1869.

Before they went their separate ways, everyone agreed they would keep in touch, and they would get together at least once a year at Thanksgiving, from now on.

The Johnsons

- Caroline was successfully treated for tuberculosis in Reno, Nevada. After she was completely healthy, she became a tour guide at the Historical Fourth Ward School Museum in Virginia City. Visitors to the museum are always impressed with her knowledge of Virginia City's history. She loves the new washer and dryer she and Bill recently purchased.

- Bill retired from his tour guide position, not wanting to risk the possibility that another earthquake could send him to the past again. He still goes out prospecting for gold, when the weather is nice.

- Bill and Caroline currently reside in Virginia City, where they are living happily ever after, in the twenty-first century. The Taylor children continue to call them "Uncle Bill and Aunt Caroline."

The Taylors

- Pete is a happy dog who thoroughly enjoys his life with the Taylor family. He loves his monthly trips to the pet groomer.

- Alex passed his CPR test and earned his Boy Scout First Aid badge. He developed a strong interest in earthquakes and spends a lot of time reading books and online articles about seismology. He and Natalie have plans to spend their next summer vacation with Uncle Bill and Aunt Caroline.

- Natalie waited for two days before shaving both sides of her head again. She joined her local swimming club and usually takes first place in their competitions. History is now her favorite subject in school.

- Benjamin spent the rest of summer chasing Pete around the backyard. In the Fall, he enrolled in first grade—for the second time. He is one of the best students in his class.

- Thomas and Mary paid off their house and plan to retire early. They would like to travel and visit new places. In the meantime, they are living their best lives and enjoying the twenty-first century.

Notes from the Author

This story focuses on a fictional family, but I have tried to present Virginia City in 1869 as truthfully as possible. Many of the events in this novel actually occurred during the timeframe that our fictional family was there. Several newspaper articles and photos included at the back of this book are images from 1869. Some events, places, and people were slightly manipulated to better fit the fictional narrative, and for that, I hope scholarly historians and purists will accept my apologies.

The Historic Fourth Ward School Museum

Go to http://fourthwardschool.org to learn more about this organization's efforts preserve the history of education in Virginia City and Nevada.

Go to https://comstockfoundation.org to learn more about this organization's efforts to preserve the history and culture of the Comstock.

Special thanks to the Chollar Mine
and the people of Virginia City, Nevada.
https://chollarminetour.com
https://visitvirginiacitynv.com

About the Author

Brenda Findley believes that a good story can take you anywhere you want to go. She holds a Doctorate in Education, and loves writing books that provide historical and factual information in an entertaining way.

Her grandchildren are the inspiration for her writing, and initially served as her entire audience. She is glad you have joined them!

For information about other books by Dr. Findley, go to brendafindley.com.

About The Co-Author

Carter Charles Chasson (also known as "C-Cubed") is Dr. Findley's grandson. At the time of this book's first publishing, he is nine years old and in the fourth grade.

In addition to helping his grandmother with this book, he likes to write his own graphic novel stories. He also enjoys reading and playing video games.

His favorite subject in school is lunch.

First Reader & Author's Editor

Zachary Chasson is Dr. Findley's eldest grandson. At the time of this book's first publishing, he is eleven years old and in the sixth grade. Zachary performed the duties of First Reader and Author's Editor for this book.

Zachary likes to play a variety of sports and enjoys playing video games. He also likes to hang out with his friends.

His least favorite food is squash.

The Author is grateful for Zachary's attention to detail and innate editorial skills.

IMAGES
from 1869

Bathing Dresses

Courtesy of the New York Public Library Picture
Collection. Exploring the History of the Swimsuit
with NYPL's Electronic Resources

PIPER'S OPERA HOUSE.

S. BLEEKER.........................Manager.
NED DAVIS ....Agent.

Positively Two Days Only!

THE ORIGINAL AND ONLY.

GENERAL TOM THUMB

AND WIFE,

—AND—

COMMODORE NUTT,

—AND—

MINNIE WARREN,

In their Beautiful Performances.

WEDNESDAY AND THURSDAY,

August 4 and 5.

The Miniature Carriage and Ponies are driven by a DWARF COACHMAN, brother to Commodore Nutt, and will parade the streets on the days of performance.

PRICES OF ADMISSION:

Dress Circle.........................$1 00
Chuildren under 10, with Parents,
  to Dress Circle 50
Parquette............................. 50
Private Boxes.................... $3 and $5
  Two performances each day, at 3 and 8 P. M.

WASHOE................Armory Hall, July 31
CARSON................Theater, August 2
DAYTON.................Odeon Hall, August 3
RENO..................Alhambra Hall, August 6
jy30–td

Piper's Opera House Advertisement #1

Gold Hill daily news. [volume] (Gold Hill, N.T. [Nev.]), 3 Aug. 1869. *Chronicling America: Historic American Newspapers.* Lib. Of Congress.

278

Piper's Opera House Advertisement #2

Gold Hill daily news. [volume] (Gold Hill, N.T. [Nev.]), 3 Aug. 1869. *Chronicling America: Historic American Newspapers.* Lib. Of Congress.

SHOEING FEAT.—At Miss Emma For-restell, the india-rubber woman's, en-tertainment last Monday evening, at Piper's Opera House, that remarkable female athlete, among other difficult feats, did one which few among the men of this section at least, would care to attempt, even if able to endure it. With her heels resting on one chair and her shoulders on another, a common sized blacksmith's anvil was placed on her chest, and there she supported it steadily for five or six minutes, while Hemenway, the well known blacksmith, brought in a red-hot horse-shoe, which he turned after the usual style, with the assistance of a striker with a sledge, finishing it off complete, nail-holes and all, just as he would in his own shop. It was a pretty severe test of her en-durance, but she stood it manfully. She afterward presented the shoe to Haight, the well known rider of the Pacific Union Express pony between Reno and Virginia, and it can be seen at the office of the company, Virginia. Haight is going to nail that shoe on the foot of his bed to keep witches and other ob-noxious intruders away.

India Rubber Woman

> BASE BALL AT CARSON.—
> The first game of base ball between the
> Virginia City Club of Virginia and the
> Silver Star Club of Carson will take
> place on Saturday next, on the Plaza in
> Carson. Play will be called at one
> o'clock P. M. As it is necessary to have
> on the day of the match, a clear field,
> persons desirous of seeing the game will
> enter the Plaza at the corner nearest
> Greenebaum's store and the entrance in
> front of the store of Mason & Huff, and
> keep within the two rows of trees on
> the north and west sides. Seats for
> ladies will be placed where a good view
> of the playing can be had. A committee
> will be upon the ground to see that
> ladies are provided with seats. The
> Plaza will be so enclosed as to keep
> cattle from the ground.

Carson City v. Virginia City Base Ball #1

The Carson daily appeal. [volume] (Carson City, Nev.), 15 Sept. 1869. *Chronicling America: Historic American Newspapers.* Lib. of Congress.

THE CARSON BASE BALL MATCH.—
The *Appeal* of this morning, in speaking
of the grand match game which takes
place to-day at Carson between the Virginia City Base Ball Club and the Silver
Star Club of that town, says that everything has been put in tip-top order for
the occasion, and a very interesting and
exciting match it will doubtless be.
Following are the names of the two
nines to play the game: Virginia City
Base Ball Club—Kelly, catcher; Beals,
pitcher; Hopkins, first base; Angell,
second base; Lackey, third base; Brady,
short stop; Crandall, left field; Wood-
burne, centre field; Campbell, right
field. Silver Star Base Ball Club—Bur-
gesser, catcher; Johnson, pitcher;
Cowan, first base; Finney, second base;
Day, third base; Berthrong, short stop;
Sharp, left field; Meder, centre field;
Parkinson, right field.

Carson City v. Virginia City Base Ball #1

Gold Hill daily news. [volume] (Gold Hill, N.T.
[Nev.]), 25 Sept. 1869. *Chronicling America:
Historic American Newspapers.* Lib. of Congress.

Virginia City Club v. Carson City Stars

Photo Courtesy of Nevada State Museum

BASE BALL TO-MORROW.—The grand Base Ball return match, at Virginia, to-morrow, between the Silver Star Club, of Carson, and the Virginia Club, is much spoken of and will be a very interesting affair. The Carson Club will be met at Gold Hill about 8 o'clock in the morning, and taken charge of as the guests of the Virginia Club, who will entertain them in true hospitable and brotherly style, intending to send them back home before they are twenty-four hours older, considerably beaten. The grounds are well prepared, and convenient seats furnished for ladies, with their escorts, like as they were at Carson when over 500 ladies witnessed the recent match game. No profanity will be allowed, but everything will be conducted in the most gentlemanly and orderly manner. Game will be called at 12 o'clock, noon, precisely, and the sport will last for three or four hours. Those who have never seen the beautiful and exciting game of base ball, had better attend to-morrow and be delighted.

Virginia City Club v. Carson City Stars

Gold Hill daily news. [volume] (Gold Hill, N.T. [Nev.]), 08 Oct. 1869. *Chronicling America: Historic American Newspapers*. Lib. of Congress.